A
―――――
CANDLELIGHT REGENCY SPECIAL

Candlelight Regencies

- 216 A GIFT OF VIOLETS, *Janette Radcliffe*
- 221 THE RAVEN SISTERS, *Dorothy Mack*
- 225 THE SUBSTITUTE BRIDE, *Dorothy Mack*
- 227 A HEART TOO PROUD, *Laura London*
- 232 THE CAPTIVE BRIDE, *Lucy Phillips Stewart*
- 239 THE DANCING DOLL, *Janet Louise Roberts*
- 240 MY LADY MISCHIEF, *Janet Louise Roberts*
- 245 LA CASA DORADA, *Janet Louise Roberts*
- 246 THE GOLDEN THISTLE, *Janet Louise Roberts*
- 247 THE FIRST WALTZ, *Janet Louise Roberts*
- 248 THE CARDROSS LUCK, *Janet Louise Roberts*
- 250 THE LADY ROTHSCHILD, *Samantha Lester*
- 251 BRIDE OF CHANCE, *Lucy Phillips Stewart*
- 253 THE IMPOSSIBLE WARD, *Dorothy Mack*
- 255 THE BAD BARON'S DAUGHTER, *Laura London*
- 257 THE CHEVALIER'S LADY, *Betty Hale Hyatt*
- 263 MOONLIGHT MIST, *Laura London*
- 501 THE SCANDALOUS SEASON, *Nina Pykare*
- 505 THE BARTERED BRIDE, *Anne Hillary*
- 512 BRIDE OF TORQUAY, *Lucy Phillips Stewart*
- 515 MANNER OF A LADY, *Cilla Whitmore*
- 521 LOVE'S CAPTIVE, *Samantha Lester*
- 527 KITTY, *Jennie Tremaine*
- 530 BRIDE OF A STRANGER, *Lucy Phillips Stewart*
- 537 HIS LORDSHIP'S LANDLADY, *Cilla Whitmore*
- 542 DAISY, *Jennie Tremaine*
- 543 THE SLEEPING HEIRESS, *Phyllis Taylor Pianka*
- 548 LOVE IN DISGUISE, *Nina Pykare*
- 549 THE RUNAWAY HEIRESS, *Lillian Cheatham*
- 554 A MAN OF HER CHOOSING, *Nina Pykare*
- 555 PASSING FANCY, *Mary Linn Roby*
- 570 THOMASINA, *Joan Vincent*
- 571 SENSIBLE CECILY, *Margaret Summerville*
- 572 DOUBLE FOLLY, *Marnie Ellingson*
- 573 POLLY, *Jennie Tremaine*

The Mismatched Lovers

Anne Hillary

A CANDLELIGHT REGENCY
SPECIAL

Published by
Dell Publishing Co., Inc.
1 Dag Hammarskjold Plaza
New York, New York 10017

Copyright © 1980 by Anne Mikita Kolaczyk

All rights reserved. No part of this book
may be reproduced or transmitted in any form
or by any means, electronic or mechanical, including
photocopying, recording or by any information storage
and retrieval system, without the written permission
of the Publisher, except where permitted by law.

Dell ® TM 681510, Dell Publishing Co., Inc.

ISBN: 0-440-16388-9

Printed in the United States of America

First printing—June 1980

No disguise can long conceal love where it is, nor feign it where it is not.

—Rochefoucauld

CHAPTER ONE

Julia thought it was just too beautiful a day to waste staying indoors. She was not at all tired by the carriage ride home and decided to spend a few hours this afternoon just enjoying King's Rest, for early tomorrow morning they were leaving for London.

She rode her horse up a nearby hill. From the top of it she could see her home, and the home of one of their neighbors: Worth Hall. She dismounted and settled herself under a large oak tree. She took off a silly-looking bonnet and tossed it on the ground. Then she shook her head, letting the breeze muss her curls into delightful disorder.

"Oh, it's good to be home," she sighed as she leaned back against the tree trunk.

"I don't suppose that's because I'm here," a man said, stepping forward from the shelter of some trees.

Julia jumped at the sound of his voice, but

settled back once she saw who it was. "Oh, hello, Marc," was all she said.

Marcus Cotsworthy had been her friend and neighbor for as long as she could remember. She enjoyed his company, but he wasn't someone to get excited about, she thought, not realizing that at twenty-five years of age he was the object of many admiring female glances. He was tall and his coat of blue broadcloth fit smoothly over his wide shoulders. His brown hair was lightened by the sun and made his brown eyes seem even darker. As if his handsome figure was not enough to attract women, his home, Worth Hall, was well furnished and comfortable, and he possessed a considerable fortune that would keep his bride in French kid gloves and Spanish lace for a long time, if he would just choose someone for that position. To Julia, however, he was just an old friend.

Marc smiled wryly at her lack of enthusiasm. It was quite a change from the false adulation of the matchmaking mothers and simpering daughters he met in London.

"It's been a long time since you were home," he said as he sat down next to her. "I've missed you."

Julia knew better than to let Marc get on a personal topic. "I didn't expect to see you here at all," she told him. "I thought you were still on the peninsula." She looked at him questioningly.

"I'm here in Somerset only for a few days," he explained, "but I've been back from the peninsula for about six months. I work for the foreign office now."

Julia did not seem satisfied with such a brief explanation, but he offered no more. "Then I won't see you in your uniform?" she asked, looking disappointed. She sighed as Marc shook his head. "That's too bad. Phoebe and I saw some soldiers on our way home from school and they looked so handsome in their uniforms. I told her that I was sure you looked just as nice in yours."

Marc wondered briefly if he could impress Julia by reenlisting, but remembering the injury that forced him out, decided that there was little he could do about it. "Has your guardian arrived yet?" he asked her.

"Oh, no," she said. "He's not coming here." Julia noticed his surprise, then laughed. "I was forgetting that you don't know the news. Phoebe and I are going to London! Lady Ffoulkes has decided that it's time we were out of school and presented to society. Isn't that exciting?"

"It seems like a good idea," Marc said, smiling. "But aren't they coming here to get you?"

"It's not necessary," Julia assured him. "Sir Giles has sent his coach. It came to school to get us. We're just here overnight, then tomorrow we leave for London! I can hardly believe it. There were times when I feared that grandfather had forgotten all about us, or meant us to stay in school forever."

"I don't think he knew what to do with you and your sister," Marc said. "He was rather set in his ways by the time you and Phoebe came to live with him."

Julia nodded. Her grandfather, Sir James Henley, had been a recluse even fourteen years ago when Julia and Phoebe had been left in his care on the death of their parents. He had made no effort to change his ways, and sent them off to boarding school as soon as they were old enough. Even after his death last year they had been forced to remain in school. A distant cousin was their only relative, and along with the baronetcy and the family estate, he inherited responsibility for the girls. Unfortunately, he was a minor government official in India, and the girls had to wait until he could return to England.

"Miss Cranmore's School for Young Ladies of Quality." Julia made a face. "I had nightmares of it turning into Miss Henley's School for Young Ladies. I could see myself as a shriveled old spinster teaching needlework and deportment to unruly girls." She shuddered visibly. "Oh, I am so glad to be free of that place."

Marc laughed at her fervor. "It couldn't have

been that bad," he said. "I was at school, too, and I can remember many good times I had there. I'm sure that you had lots of friends."

"Not anymore," she said. "I'm eighteen now. All my friends left long ago. They've had seasons in London, and some of them are already married." Julia stopped abruptly, realizing the opening she had given him.

"You could be married by now, too, if you wanted to be," Marc said quietly. "As a matter of fact, if you say yes now, we could be married by the end of the month." He looked at her hopefully.

"Oh, Marc," Julia said angrily as she stood up. "Why do you always have to spoil everything? We used to be good friends and have fun together. Like the times you taught me to ride, or when we hid from your father in the apple trees, or the time you took that bottle of wine out of your father's cellar and we got so sick from it." Marc had the grace to look chagrined at that. "Lately, though, you always seem to spoil our good times."

"There are other ways of having a good time," Marc said as he stood next to her. "I think we're both a little old to be climbing trees."

"That's not the point," Julia insisted. "You're a good friend, and I do like you, but I don't want to marry you."

"I don't think you know what you want," he

pointed out reasonably. "You've been cooped up in school far too long. You're old enough to be married, but you still think like a schoolgirl."

"I do not," Julia cried, "and I am capable of making up my own mind. Why can't you just forget all this nonsense and go find some other girl to keep house for you?"

"I wasn't asking you to marry me because I think you'd be a good housekeeper," he said, losing patience with her. "There's a bit more to marriage than keeping the linen mended."

Julia blushed, and as she walked away from him, Marc continued in a quieter tone. "You know that I love you, and I think you could love me, too, if you'd give yourself a chance. You're eighteen already. You don't have forever to make up your mind about me, or you'll be left on the shelf."

As soon as the words came out of his mouth, Marc knew he had made a mistake. Julia pulled herself up to her full height, which was still quite a bit shorter than he was, and marched back to where he was standing.

"I'll have you know that I have no intention of being an old maid," she said. "When I go to London, I'm going to meet someone terribly handsome, maybe an earl or a duke, and we're going to fall in love and I'll marry him. I don't know why you think I'll never marry if I don't marry you. There are other men in the world, you know.

And you're older than I am, so you're the one who doesn't have any time to lose. You'd better start looking for that other girl, or you'll be the one left on the shelf."

Julia pushed past him and gave him a fierce look that only made him laugh. She ran over to her horse, anxious to get away, but realized as she looked up at her saddle that it wasn't going to be that easy. She was going to need his help, or have to walk home.

Looking over her shoulder, she saw that Marc was enjoying her predicament. "Aren't you going to help me?" she asked, trying to sound meek but not coming too close to it.

"Maybe we could make a bargain," he suggested as he casually walked over. She looked at him suspiciously.

"I'll help you back on your horse," he offered innocently, "for a kiss."

"I'll walk home first," Julia said angrily.

But Marc just laughed and, putting his hands around her waist, lifted her up. He gave her a quick kiss on the cheek before he put her in the saddle. "Welcome home, Julia!" he called to her as she stormed away.

Marc watched as she rode down the hill toward her home. Earls and dukes, indeed! he laughed. Most of the earls and dukes that were present in London these days were gouty old men. Not quite the sort to set a young girl's heart aflame with love. A few days in town should dispel that dream—then he would give her a chance to change her mind about him.

Early the next morning a coach was slowly making its way along the muddy roads of western Somerset.

"At this rate it'll be midnight before we arrive," moaned Phoebe.

"You knew it would take us almost all day," Julia reminded her. "No matter how hard you wish us there, we won't get to London before this evening."

Phoebe stirred restlessly in her seat. Although she did know how long it would take them, she hadn't resigned herself to the whole day being spent in travel. She sat in silence for a few minutes. "I don't know how you can be so calm," Phoebe finally said to Julia, "when we'll be in London tonight."

Julia laughed. "I don't feel very calm," she assured her sister. "If I thought it would help, I'd get out and push the carriage along to make it move faster."

An older servant named Meg was escorting the girls. Since she had looked after them whenever they had stayed at their grandfather's house, she had no hesitation about speaking her mind.

"Just enjoy the peace while ye can," she advised them. "By next week ye'll be wishing for a day of quiet."

"Not me," Phoebe vowed. "I'll never get tired of going to parties and balls and everything." She sighed as she pictured herself surrounded by admirers, begging for the honor of a dance with her. "I shall want to dance until morning every night," she told them.

Since Julia herself had similar dreams, she just smiled in agreement, but Meg was clearly not impressed. "And just what do ye know 'bout dancing all night?" she snorted in disgust. "The only dancing ye've done has been in school. And that's a bit different than a party. Yer going to be tired, ye'll see."

Phoebe knew that Meg just did not understand, but rather than argue, she turned to look out the window again, hoping to be surprised at the distance they had covered.

"Are you staying with us in London?" Julia asked Meg. "Or do you have to return to Somerset?"

"I don't know her ladyship's plans, but I might be stayin'." She looked over at Phoebe who was lost in her dreams again. "Somebody'll have to look out fer the two of ye."

"Do you suppose that we'll go somewhere this evening?" Phoebe asked Julia, forgetting Meg's unsympathetic attitude.

Julia shook her head. "I doubt it. And I don't want too many people to see me until I've gotten some new clothes." She looked down in dismay at the traveling gown she was wearing. It had been fine for traveling back and forth from school, but it was hardly what a lady of fashion would choose to be seen in, since it made her look about twelve years old.

"That's true," Phoebe agreed. "I don't think that too many handsome young men would notice us dressed as we are. Just think, Julia, we'll have all the latest styles with ruffles and lace and ribands. We'll look just beautiful."

"Beauty is as beauty does," Meg said darkly, but neither girl paid much attention to her.

"I think I better stay with the simpler styles," Julia sighed. "I don't look as pretty as you do in the fussier ones."

"Nonsense," Phoebe insisted. "Why we're practically identical. We both look good in the same styles."

Julia wished it were true. Phoebe was small and fragile looking. Her hair was a pale blond that never seemed to get mussed. She had pale skin and bright blue eyes. She looked quite appealing in the light colors that young girls were supposed to wear, and Julia was sure that Phoebe would break many hearts once they were settled in London.

Although she and Phoebe were about the same

18

height, the resemblance ended there. Julia's chestnut-brown hair was cut short and curled much too freely, which made it difficult to force into the current styles. She had dark blue eyes that were large and heavily fringed. She looked sadly down at her trim waist and full breasts, which couldn't be disguised, however hard she tried. She just could not be pleased with her looks, for no matter how pleasing Marc Cotsworthy seemed to think they were, Julia knew that they were just not in fashion.

"We wouldn't want to be dressed exactly the same, anyway," Phoebe added. "Because then all those handsome men wouldn't know who they were proposing to."

Julia laughed quite happily. "We'll have such fun in London. I just wish that we had a whole season there."

"We'll have more than a month in London," Phoebe pointed out. "And from there maybe we'll go to Bath or Brighton, or one of the resorts. Once we're a part of society, we'll be expected to go to all those places."

But Julia was not so sure. "I don't know if Lady Ffoulkes is going to want to take us all those places."

"Oh, she'll only take us to the first few," Phoebe assured her. "After that we'll be married to some devastatingly handsome men who are madly in love with us. They'll take us where we want to go." She sighed contentedly and leaned back against the rich velvet squabs.

The girls drifted into silence as the rocking of the coach and the monotonous scenery lulled them to sleep.

Before very long they were awake again. The coach was no longer moving and seemed to be standing at a very strange angle.

"Jem," Julia called to the coachman. "What's wrong?"

His face appeared at the window. "Nothin' ta worry 'bout!" he assured them good-naturedly. "Just a bit too much mud in the road."

Phoebe gave a cry of despair as she leaned out of the window on her side of the coach. "A little too much mud!" she moaned. "We're practically buried in it!"

"Oo, it ain't that bad," Jem smiled, but Phoebe looked at him darkly, as if he was plotting against their arrival in town. "I'll have you out in a wink," he assured her. But the wink proved to be a rather long one. He eventually reappeared at the window, still quite cheerful. "Might help if you ladies was to step down fer a spell," he suggested.

Phoebe scrambled out of the coach, glad to do anything that might help them be on their way, but she was not so pleased when she looked up at the sky. "It's going to rain," she told Jem. "We can't stay here."

Jem looked up at the sky, which had grown quite dark. Thunder was rumbling ominously in the distance. "It ain't gonna rain fer a spell yet," he said positively.

Julia hoped that the storm heard him, for she had no desire to get soaked either. Meg was trying to take charge of the girls, but had a fear of thunder and lightning and jumped at every sound.

Jem's optimism did not help move the coach, though he kept trying. The storm was moving closer and Julia could feel the ground tremble with the force of it.

"Oh, Jem, we'll get soaked," Phoebe wailed. "Can't we get back inside?"

Julia agreed with Phoebe, as the trembling of the ground increased. Suddenly, another coach rounded the corner, and Julia realized with relief that it was the coach, not the storm, that had caused the ground to tremble. The carriage stopped next to them and Julia looked up at the occupant. It was a man in his late thirties, dressed in the height of fashion in a gray wool coat that fit without a wrinkle. His trousers were buff colored, his waistcoat a magnificent deep red. Above it was an immaculate cravat, tied in an intricate style that Julia had never seen before. He had light hair and beautiful green eyes. He was altogether the most splendid person she had ever seen, except that all this perfection was marred slightly by the coldness of his eyes, which were not touched by the smile on his lips.

"Do you need some help?" he asked her.

Meg was sure that they should not accept help from this stranger, but the girls did not wait for her to answer.

"Our coach is struck in the mud," Julia explained.

"And we're going to get wet," Phoebe added.

"That doesn't seem to be too hard to fix," he said pleasantly, and Julia chided herself for thinking him cold. He turned to his tiger riding at the back of the curricle. "Ben, help get the coach out," he said curtly, then turned back to the ladies. "I'll take you ahead to the Golden Goose where you can wait for your carriage."

His take-charge attitude was too much for Meg who decided that getting wet was better than being abducted by a strange man. She placed herself protectively in front of the girls. "There ain't nobody goin' no place," she announced. "We can all wait here, while yer Ben helps Jem, thank you."

The gentleman looked far from pleased. "I do not intend to let a two-hundred-guinea coat be ruined because you think we should all wait here."

Meg turned red at his tone of voice, but was not about to give in. "You can go to the Golden Goose, then," she offered. "We'll bring Ben along when we're done."

"I have better things to do with my time than bandy words with an impertinent servant," he said quietly but with force. "I shall indeed wait out the storm at the inn, but I shall have Ben with me, so we can resume our journey without delay." He looked over to where Ben was helping Jem.

The girls were sure they were to be stranded unless they could stop Meg. "Don't be so silly, Meg," Phoebe said quickly. "We'll come to no harm." She turned to the gentleman who was watching them with no apparent interest in the outcome.

"We'd be very grateful if you would escort us to the inn," Phoebe said politely, ignoring Meg's shocked cry.

He nodded and stepped down to help the girls into his curricle. "We'll have to hurry if we are to stay dry," he warned them as the horses began.

They raced down the road, with the girls clinging to the sides so they wouldn't be thrown out. It was with some relief that they reached the inn and were shown into a private parlor.

"Perhaps we should introduce ourselves," the gentleman suggested. "I am Sir Tristan Bentley."

"I am Miss Julia Henley," Julia said uncertainly. She had rather mixed feelings about this man. He had been quite polite to Phoebe and herself, but she was puzzled by his rudeness to Meg and his own servant. Perhaps, though, that was how most people treated their servants, Julia thought, and allowed herself to forget her doubts under the persuasion of his smile. He was so splendidly handsome that Julia could only marvel that he had bothered to stop and help them at all.

Sir Tristan ordered tea for them, and Phoebe spent the time they were waiting happily telling him about their trip to London, while Julia sat back and wondered if he was really as interested as he seemed to be, or was he merely being courteous.

By the time the tea arrived, and Julia began to pour it out, at Sir Tristan's request, Phoebe was plying him with questions about London. She was disappointed that he could not tell her all the kinds of animals that were housed at the Royal Exchange.

Then, momentarily out of questions, Phoebe put her cup down and looked around. "This is quite lovely," she said, referring to the parlor they were in. It was small and furnished with plain, wooden settees and a low table. The floor was covered partially with a knotted rug whose bright colors were reflected in the curtains that hung over the windows, blocking out the storm. She turned back to Sir Tristan.

"Do you go to many parties in London?" she asked suddenly.

"A few," he admitted.

"Perhaps we'll see you at some of them," Julia smiled shyly.

Sir Tristan nodded, but privately thought it most unlikely. He doubted that they would frequent the gaming halls that he enjoyed, and his time at respectable gatherings was quite used up by any new heiress that happened along.

He had already noted the girls' shabby clothing and felt that little would be gained by furthering this chance acquaintance. He knew, though, that appearances could be deceiving and since he kept watching for his big chance, he hid his impatience to be gone.

"Did it really cost you two hundred guineas?" Phoebe asked, breaking into his thoughts. "Your coat," she added, seeing his blank look. "You told Meg it cost that much."

"Close to it," he admitted with a smile that was due to the fact that so far the coat had cost him nothing, since he had conveniently overlooked the bill for several months.

"Are you girls staying with your parents in town?" he asked.

"Oh, no," Phoebe explained. "Our parents died years ago. We're going to stay with our guardian, Sir Giles Ffoulkes."

Sir Tristan shook his head. "That name isn't familiar to me, I'm afraid."

"Sir Giles just inherited the titles from our grandfather," Julia told him. "He was Sir James Henley. You may have heard of him."

He hadn't but did not want to appear so unknowing. "I have heard the name," he said.

"He stayed out in the country for years," Phoebe said disgustedly. "He never even went into London to go to the theater."

"Were you girls his only relatives?" he pried a bit more.

"Just us and Sir Giles," Julia answered.

"Sir Giles got the estate," Phoebe confided, "and we got the money."

"Phoebe!" Julia admonished her. It wasn't the thing to say to a complete stranger, however charming he might be.

"Well, it's true," Phoebe insisted. "He didn't even know Sir Giles, so why would he leave him all his money?"

Julia sighed and received a sympathetic smile from Sir Tristan. She wondered how she could have thought his eyes were cold, for there was no trace of coldness now. Perhaps it was just his manner with strangers, she told herself, glad that he did not appear to be shocked at Phoebe's forthrightness. She feared she had better have a long talk with her sister before she made everyone in London think they were heiresses. After all, grandfather's fortune had been quite small by the time he died. It made a comfortable dowry of five thousand pounds for each of them, with some extra for their expenses during their season.

"It was quite generous of him to leave his fortune equally to you two," Sir Tristan said innocently as he warmed up to the girls. "I've heard of some people who give all their money to one relative, while completely ignoring another." He made it sound like a shameful thing to do.

"Well, actually," Phoebe confided again. "Julia does get a bit more than me. Not much. But she is the eldest, you know."

Julia was ready to gag Phoebe by this time. The little bit more that Phoebe spoke of was an extra hundred pounds that her grandfather had set aside for his first grandchild. She thought he probably had forgotten it was there.

Julia heard a carriage approaching and was quite relieved to see it was theirs.

"Our carriage is here," she told Phoebe, who looked disappointed. "Thank you so much for everything," Julia told Sir Tristan. "We are truly in your debt."

"It was my pleasure, Miss Henley," he assured her.

"Good-bye," Phoebe said. "I do hope we will see you in London." She looked quickly over at Julia who was trying to usher her out the door before she said something else that she shouldn't.

"Don't worry," Sir Tristan smiled at her. "I don't intend to let such lovely ladies disappear from my life. I can promise that I will see you again."

Phoebe smiled and went over as Meg came rushing in. She looked quite relieved to see the girls apparently safe, and hurried Phoebe out to the coach as Julia followed more slowly.

"I would like to apologize for my sister," Julia said quietly. "She says far more than she should. I hope you were not offended by her."

Sir Tristan took her hand. "How could I be? She is a delightful child," he said, putting the emphasis on "child." Julia smiled at him as she repeated her thanks.

"I am the one in your debt for the pleasant conversation," he assured her, and lifted her hand to his lips for a brief kiss.

As the coach pulled away Sir Tristan remained in the doorway, staring after it. His luck at cards had been very bad lately and his luck with the wealthy women in town had been even worse. It seemed that fortune was finally smiling on him, though, for he was one of the first to meet these two heiresses. He must find a way to remind them of the service he had paid them, he thought, and take advantage of their gratitude as soon as possible.

Inside the coach Phoebe leaned over, close to Julia. "Wasn't he handsome?" she whispered excitedly. "It was just like a dream. A beautiful stranger came to our rescue when we were in peril. He took one look and fell in love," she sighed.

"But there were two of us," Julia laughed.

"Which one captured his fancy?" She was fairly sure she knew the answer.

"It doesn't matter," Phoebe said, shrugging it aside. "There will be so many others in London that are just as handsome and rich that we'll both have our pick."

CHAPTER TWO

The small town house on Bolton Street did not look ostentatious from the outside, but the inside had been lavishly refurnished. Only the brightly polished knocker that had been put back up on the door told that the house had undergone a change in fortunes.

Sir Giles, due to his advantageous marriage, had no lack of money to spend on his London residence. Even the attics where the maids slept had received new coats of paint and new mattresses. (The latter was due more to necessity than a desire to make living conditions more pleasant.) He spared no expense on his and Lady Ffoulkes's apartments and on the sitting and dining rooms on the first floor. If he was a little less extravagant with the furnishings of the guest rooms, it still could not be said that they were drab.

The entrance hall was his special pride. The walls were hung with gold velvet and crowded with paintings and sculptures. It was overpowering, as Julia and Phoebe discovered when they entered the house.

The accident with the carriage had delayed them, and when they finally arrived, they discovered that neither Sir Giles nor Lady Ffoulkes were at home. The housekeeper showed them to their rooms and sent them some supper. They both retired to bed soon afterward.

Julia had been given a small room at the back of the house. It was done in blue and cream with touches of peach. Because of the size of the room, there was space for only a bed, a dressing table, a wardrobe, and a small chair, but it was so delightfully arranged that Julia did not feel cramped.

Phoebe was across the hall. Her room was quite similar in size and furniture, but the predominant color was green. At the end of the hall there was a small sitting room that the housekeeper had told the girls had been set aside for their use.

It was not until the next morning that they met Lady Ffoulkes. As they were dressing, Meg came in with a message that they were to go to Lady Ffoulkes's apartment before breakfast. The girls were quite anxious to hear the particulars of their season, so they finished dressing quickly and hurried off to meet Lady Ffoulkes.

The girls were shown into a large room that was dominated by a massive bed. The heavy darkness of the wood was partially hidden by the pink curtains that hung around it, but could be seen at the corners where a golden cupid held the curtains back. In the middle of the bed sat a large woman. She wore a pink dressing gown that was trimmed in gold. A lace cap hid most of her hair, but a few gray strands had managed to slip down. Across her lap was a tray bearing her breakfast.

She looked up as the girls entered and wiped her mouth with a pink napkin. "I am Lady Ffoulkes," she told them, beckoning them impatiently forward. "Who is the oldest?" she asked.

"I am," Julia said as she came a little closer. Lady Ffoulkes looked her over carefully, then turned to Phoebe.

"Come closer, gel, will you?" she said irritably. "I can't see you if you hide back there."

Phoebe stepped closer to Julia and waited while Lady Ffoulkes looked her up and down, as if she was weighing her good points against her faults.

Finally Lady Ffoulkes shook her head. "I guess you could be worse," she muttered to herself. She indicated two chairs pulled up next to the bed and went back to her breakfast. After several eggs, a large helping of kidneys, and a thick slice of bread covered with butter, she leaned back against her pillows and looked at the girls.

"You may as well know why I brought you to London," she said, pausing to pour herself a cup of tea. She took a long drink, then put the cup down. "I don't intend to spend my time mothering two girls who are old enough to have families of their own. I don't know what your grandfather was thinking of, but you both should have been married by now." She took another sip of her tea and waved to her maid to take the tray away.

"Sir Giles has accepted the responsibility for you girls for the present time, but it isn't an arrangement to our liking. We have other interests that we wish to be free to pursue. So during the next month I shall expect each one of you to find a husband." She picked up the mail that had been left on her bed and began to browse through it.

Both girls had come to London with the expectation that they would find husbands, but they had not expected that it would be made mandatory. Suddenly the month seemed very short.

"You mean we have to find a husband during the next month?" Julia asked.

Lady Ffoulkes looked up from her mail. "That's what I said, wasn't it? Surely, you two don't expect Sir Giles and me to support you forever."

"No, no," Julia mumbled hastily. "We hadn't expected that."

"What if no one offers for us?" Phoebe asked timidly.

"That won't happen," Lady Ffoulkes assured her. "You girls have modest dowries and, with the proper clothes, you'll be fairly attractive. It shouldn't be too hard to settle you respectably. If it seems that no one is about to offer, I have a few prospects that will be happy to oblige me by marrying you."

The girls sat in silence, trying to digest everything that Lady Ffoulkes had told them. Julia thought she saw one glimmer of hope.

"If there was someone we were rather partial to, then you would have no objection to us marrying him?" she asked.

Phoebe looked at Lady Ffoulkes hopefully.

"If he makes an offer first, it's fine with me. But we don't intend to pass up others in the hope that your choice might come to the sticking point."

The girls both sighed in relief. At least they weren't to be forced into marrying someone they despised. Not if they could find someone better in the allotted time.

Lady Ffoulkes saw their relief and warned them. "As long as he's respectable and you don't do anything scandalous to attract his interest, I don't care who you marry. But I mean to have you married by the end of the season. Remember that. If you can't bring someone to the sticking point, I will." She let that thought sink in, then waved them out the door. "Go have some breakfast and get ready to go shopping. We've got a lot to buy before you can go anywhere."

An hour later the girls were waiting in the hall for Lady Ffoulkes. In spite of the news of their impending marriages, both girls were excited at the idea of getting new clothes. Julia was still a bit worried, though.

"Our season isn't going to be what we had hoped," Julia whispered to Phoebe.

"Yes it is," Phoebe assured her. "We're here and we have a whole month of parties, dances, and trips to the theater. It's going to be very exciting."

"We also have to find husbands," Julia reminded her.

"That was part of our plan anyway, wasn't it?" Phoebe said. "At least it was what I was hoping for. I have no desire to be left on the shelf season after season."

"But we only have one month to do it," Julia pointed out. "It takes some girls two or three seasons to find someone."

"Oh, Julia, we already met one handsome man before we even arrived here," Phoebe laughed. "Think how many more are just waiting out there, ready to fall in love with us."

Julia could not help but be infected by Phoebe's positiveness. By the time Lady Ffoulkes came down the stairs, both girls were happily anticipating the next few weeks.

Lady Ffoulkes was dressed in purple satin, trimmed in red lace, and the girls had feared that she might dress them in the same manner, but they needn't have worried for she knew just what to choose for them. Phoebe got pale colors. The slightly brighter ones were for Julia. They both got a number in white, but she was careful to select only the fabrics that would complement their coloring.

The girls stood for hours as different styles and fabrics were approved or rejected. Phoebe gave a sigh of relief as they left the dressmakers, only to learn that they were far from finished.

"We still have to get hats, gloves, stockings, fans, shoes, and shawls. There's no end to the things you need," Lady Ffoulkes told them as they trailed along behind her.

By the time they left a small shop on the Strand, the girls were much happier. Phoebe had chosen a Norwich shawl that she had fallen in love with, and Julia had a bright yellow sunshade. It would match a yellow and white cambric walking dress that she had ordered.

As they climbed into the carriage again, Julia was picturing herself strolling through the park on the arm of a handsome gentleman while all the ladies looked on in envy. That the man she pictured happened to resemble Sir Tristan was just a coincidence.

"I don't think I'll ever be able to wear all those lovely dresses," Phoebe sighed as the carriage pulled into the middle of the road. "When will we have our first chance to meet people?" she asked Lady Ffoulkes.

"I've arranged a small party early next week and

you will be able to meet some of the influential people in society there."

Phoebe looked crestfallen. "But that's so long from now," she complained. "Can't we go anywhere sooner?"

"You can't go anywhere until you've been introduced to society," Lady Ffoulkes said coldly. "And your new clothes won't be ready until then, so we couldn't move the party forward."

Phoebe's excitement had lent her a boldness that she didn't normally have, but Lady Ffoulkes's scolding had taken all of it away. She turned and quietly watched the people that they were passing. Suddenly, Phoebe gave a happy cry. "Look, Julia! There's Marc!"

Julia turned, quite surprised to see him riding along with some friends. She had somehow thought he was still in Somerset. Of course, if she had time to come to London, then so had he.

Marc rode over to the side of their carriage, followed by two other men on horseback, and introductions were made.

The smaller of Marc's two friends was Sir Archibald Muffin. He was shorter than the other two men and was dressed very quietly. He grimaced as Marc said his full name and asked to be called Muffin. He seemed very pleasant, but aside from acknowledging the introductions, he said almost nothing. He seemed content to just gaze at Phoebe.

Lt. John Lyndon was Marc's other companion.

He was tall, husky, and very friendly. He asked the girls about their impressions of the town so far and mentioned some things that they should not fail to see. Julia gave him her undivided attention.

Marc could not fail to notice how entranced Julia seemed to be with the lieutenant, and remembered her previous comments about men in uniform. He decided to ease himself into the conversation, lest she forget he was there.

Before he was able to do this, though, a sweet melodious voice could be heard above the others. "Why, Mr. Cotsworthy, how delightful to see you!"

Everyone stopped talking and turned to see who the speaker was. Sitting on horseback near the men, Julia saw a vision of loveliness. She was a young girl with raven black hair and pale skin. Her blue eyes looked almost too large to be real, and Julia wondered if she had a speck of dirt in one, for her lashes were fluttering most peculiarly. A tiny glove floated out toward Marc, who held it gently for a moment.

"It's so nice to see you again," the vision said softly. "I hope I didn't interrupt anything, but I just had to say hello." She blinked over at the girls, but dismissed them as unimportant.

Marc introduced the vision as Lady Annabella Tippet. Although she acknowledged the introductions politely, it was clear that she was only interested in Marc. She left very shortly.

"They never leave you alone, do they?" Lt. Lyndon laughed as Lady Annabella disappeared among the other people riding along the street. The lieutenant turned to the girls, laughing. "Everywhere we go crowds of beautiful girls surround him," he told them. "Poor Muffin and I are just ignored. That's why I'm so glad to see you girls here. You obviously aren't besotted by his money or his good looks, which I can assure you are only surface deep. Now maybe Muffin and I will have partners for some of the dances."

Marc would have cheerfully throttled the lieutenant by this time, for he was quite aware of the fact that Julia was not overly fond of him, and he didn't need to have the fact pointed out to him. Or have it made to seem that he flitted from girl to girl.

"It's not my fault they can't resist me," Marc said, making an attempt at humor. "But you have to admit that I don't give them any encouragement."

"That's true," the lieutenant agreed. "All the while you are dancing with the beauties of the season, you are thinking only of the one girl who has stolen your heart, whoever she may be." He leaned over toward Phoebe and Julia. "At least that's what he always wants us to believe."

Julia and Phoebe joined the others in their laughter, but Julia could feel herself blushing and refused to meet Marc's eyes. She was quite relieved when Lady Ffoulkes decided it was time to move on.

Every morning the girls were expected to present themselves in Lady Ffoulkes's room to receive any instructions about their day. The day after meeting Marc and his friends, Lady Ffoulkes was full of plans for the small party she was giving for the girls.

"We'll have it Sunday night," she told them between mouthfuls of steak. She quickly finished the rest of the meat, and the eggs, and pulled some papers off a small table nearby. "I have invited some of my friends, but we could include some of yours, if you wish."

She looked up at the girls, but neither seemed to know what she expected. "Is there anyone that we should be including? School friends? Neighbors? Anyone who might be in a position to invite you some place?"

"Maybe the Haywoods," Julia tentatively suggested. "Mr. and Mrs. Martin Haywood. They are presenting their daughter Claudia this year. She and Mr. Cotsworthy are cousins," she added.

Lady Ffoulkes nodded and added the name to her list. "How about Mr. Cotsworthy and his friends? They seemed quite anxious to know you."

Julia nodded reluctantly. She had finally come all the way to London and wanted to meet some new people, not see the same ones from back home.

"We'll have the Sigsbys," Lady Ffoulkes continued. "And Harold."

"Harold?" Phoebe asked.

"My nephew. He's been looking for a wife." She saw the girls exchange looks. "Don't forget the reason that you're here," she warned them. "I mean to get you both married, and soon." She waved the girls out of the room as her maid began to help her dress.

Coming down for breakfast the day of the party, the girls finally met Sir Giles. He was a short, reserved man. His clothes were expensive looking, and he seemed quite proud of his elegance. He stood up and smiled as the girls entered.

"It's a pleasure to meet at last," he said. "I hope you are enjoying your stay here."

"Yes, thank you," Phoebe answered.

The girls went to the sideboard to select their food, and Sir Giles resumed his study of the *Gazette*. As soon as they were finished, he put it down.

"I hear you have been getting some new clothes," he said. The girls nodded. "I expect you'll cause quite a stir with the young men tonight," he laughed.

Phoebe smiled. "We certainly hope to."

Sir Giles smiled back. "How are you getting along with Primrose?" he asked. "She's quite a lady, isn't she?" When he saw the girls' blank faces, he explained. "Primrose. Lady Ffoulkes. My wife."

"Oh, yes," Julia assured him. "We seem to get along just fine," she added hastily.

"It was certainly my lucky day when she agreed to marry me," he told the girls. "Never could understand why she picked me. She was the widow of Mr. Robert Styson." He looked up as if that name should mean something to the girls. "Well, he was a rich old coot," he laughed. "Didn't even know how much money he had, and left it all to Primrose. She could have had her pick of all the men in England," he sighed, "but she chose me. I think she had a yen to be Lady Ffoulkes," he whispered. "The title always gets them, and I knew it would come sooner or later."

Julia couldn't help smiling. He seemed so pleased that he had managed to marry Lady Ffoulkes! She couldn't imagine many men willing to take on such a domineering wife, no matter how much money she had.

"Do you like what we've done with the house?" he asked them.

"We never saw it before," Phoebe reminded him. "I don't think grandfather used it very much."

"It was very run down when we came," Sir Giles

42

admitted. "But we managed to get it into good condition for your party. Don't have to hide any of the rooms from the guests," he teased.

"It really is very nice," Julia told him, looking around the dining room. It was furnished in red and gold. A bit too bright for her tastes, but it was certainly elegant. Even the velvet covers on the chairs were rich looking. "Have you seen King's Rest yet?" Julia asked him.

King's Rest was their grandfather's home in Somerset. It had been built around 1510 by an ancestor of Julia's. It was a pleasant house for the times. Then, in 1539, Henry VIII had spent a night there, after the destruction of Glastonbury Abbey. From that time on it was known as King's Rest, and it soon began to change. An elaborate copy of Henry's coat of arms was put in plaster above the front door, but very little of it was left by this time.

Each new owner made the changes that he felt were necessary to make it look like the place where a king had rested. Massive porticos, supported by huge columns, were added to every door. Whole wings were added in whatever was the current style at the time—classical Roman, Palladian, and even a flavor of decadent baroque. The changes were mostly external, however, and the family finances usually ran out before the projects were completed, so few modern conveniences were added for the comfort of the inhabitants. The whole house was drafty and damp, some of the newer sections being far worse than the oldest parts.

"No, I haven't been there yet," Sir Giles sighed. "What's it like?"

Phoebe laughed. "It's horrid," she said. "Cold, drafty, and far too big."

But Sir Giles did not look upset. "It sounds like a challenge."

"That it'll be," Julia agreed. "Grandfather never bothered with it, and it needs a great deal of work, but I guess it is livable as it is," she hesitated. "After all, we did stay there occasionally."

"Well, when I get through with it, it will be much more livable."

The girls laughed and got up to leave the table. As they went into the hallway, Julia thought how much easier Sir Giles was to talk to than his wife. She wondered if he was as eager to see them married as Lady Ffoulkes had said.

Sir Giles was going into the library when Julia decided to see how he felt about their presence in the house. "Sir Giles?" she called after him. "Could I speak with you for a moment?"

If he was surprised by her request, Sir Giles was far too gentlemanly to show it. He stepped aside and let her enter the room first, closing the door after them.

Once she was in the room, Julia was not sure how to proceed. "It's about Lady Ffoulkes's plan to get us married quickly," she began. "Phoebe and I are rather worried about it."

"You don't want to get married?" he asked in surprise.

"Oh no, that's not it," she assured him. "It's just that we have to choose someone so fast. A month is very little time in which to choose a husband."

He nodded. "Yes, it is. It's hard to judge what someone is like in that short a time."

Julia had never imagined that he would agree with her so quickly! "We've already been here almost a week and we haven't really seen anyone. Once we are introduced at the party tonight, we will meet some more men, but we still might not meet someone we would want to marry."

"I hadn't thought of that," Sir Giles smiled. "Supposing the man who would be right for you is out of town for a few weeks, or is not invited to the same events as you. Neither of you would realize just how well suited you are."

Julia smiled in relief. "I wasn't sure you would agree with me," she laughed. "Lady Ffoulkes has not given us much chance to tell her our feelings about all this."

Sir Giles shook his head. "I'm sure that she would have understood if you had just told her. She isn't all that difficult to approach, you know."

Julia did not want to argue the matter, so she just laughed at her hesitation.

"I'll tell her myself, shall I?" he offered, and

Julia readily agreed, thinking that now she could really enjoy the parties they went to, for she could wait for someone she would love rather than just marry the first person who asked her.

"I'll tell her to use her own judgment," Sir Giles was saying. "I'm quite sure that you'll be pleased with her choices." Sir Giles was opening the door for her to leave, but Julia hadn't noticed.

"Her choices?" she repeated. "What choices?"

"Your husbands," he told her. "That was what you said, wasn't it? To have her choose for you?"

"Oh, no," Julia cried, aghast. "That's not what I meant."

"You said you couldn't make a choice in a month," Sir Giles pointed out. "I assumed that since you did not feel able to choose that you wanted us to choose for you."

"I had hoped you would let us have more time to decide," Julia explained.

"But why would you want more time?" he asked, quite puzzled. "There's only a month left of the season. What good would an extra week or so be? There'd be no one left in town by that time, and you don't have the wardrobe to go to Brighton or one of the resorts."

Julia said nothing. She just stood there looking at him, realizing for the first time just how trapped she and Phoebe were. Sir Giles was their legal guardian and he could agree to any marriage he wanted for them.

"I'm sorry," he said. "Lady Ffoulkes does know what is for the best. If you feel after a week or so that you won't be able to choose, just tell her. She'll find someone for you."

Julia turned to walk out the door. "You know," he reminded her gently, "she didn't have to invite you here at all. She could have just made arrangements for your marriage while you were still at school."

Julia nodded. "I know. We really are glad to be here. It's just that we had hoped for more time to decide."

"If he's respectable and has the money to support you, what is there to decide?" Sir Giles asked.

Julia shook her head. She knew he would not understand that she and Phoebe wanted to marry for love. They had better make good use of their month, for Sir Giles was certainly not going to help them.

CHAPTER THREE

Julia looked at herself in the mirror, rather pleased with what she saw. It was the night of their party and she had chosen a cream-colored velvet dress to wear. It was a very simple style that hung loosely from a high waistline. The neckline and hem were trimmed with embroidery of small golden flowers. Around her neck Julia wore a gold locket that had been her mother's. She had a few other pieces of jewelry, but none that went quite as well with her dress. Her hair was swept back from her face with a cream-colored riband and her curls fell loosely about.

Julia stepped back, wishing she was looking forward to the evening more. Phoebe was so excited about the whole idea of being in London, but Julia could not forget why they were there. She sighed and went to see if Phoebe was ready to go downstairs.

Phoebe was still uncertain as to which necklace

she should wear. There were several lying on her dressing table and Meg stood by holding two more.

"Oh, Julia, none of them look right," she moaned when her sister entered the room. "Maybe I shouldn't wear this dress after all."

Julia laughed as she noticed two other dresses lying on the bed. "It doesn't seem to have been your first choice."

Meg shook her head. "She just can't make up her mind."

"Stand up, Phoebe, and let's see how you look," Julia told her. "You'll have Meg wishing she had never left King's Rest."

Phoebe's dress was cream-colored also, but a much softer fabric than Julia's. It had an underskirt of pale pink, which matched the ribands that trimmed the small sleeves. Phoebe also had a pink riband in her hair. She looked quite lovely and Julia suddenly felt dissatisfied with her own appearance.

"What can't you decide about?" Julia asked her. "You look very pretty."

"But what should I wear around my neck?" she asked, holding up a string of pearls, a locket similar to Julia's, and a rather gaudy set of amethysts that she had received from her godmother.

"The pearls," Julia suggested.

"But everybody wears pearls," Phoebe complained. "Oh, if I only had some diamonds or rubies," she said wistfully.

"None of them would go as well with your dress as the pearls, anyway," Julia pointed out practically, "so put them on and let's go downstairs."

Phoebe did as she was told. "Who's coming for dinner?" she asked, taking a last look at herself in the mirror.

"Just some friends of Lady Ffoulkes's," Julia told her impatiently. "I don't remember if she even mentioned their names. Oh, do hurry, Phoebe. We mustn't be late."

"Ah, here they are now," Lady Ffoulkes said as the girls entered the drawing room.

Two young men stood up, and Julia noticed an older lady sitting near Lady Ffoulkes.

"Sybil," Lady Ffoulkes said to the lady near her, "these are Giles's wards, Julia and Phoebe." Turning to the girls, she added, "this is Mrs. Sigsby, an old friend of mine."

The girls curtsied politely, but Mrs. Sigsby only nodded coldly.

Lady Ffoulkes turned to one of the young men. He was dressed very fashionably, although he looked a little uncomfortable. His yellow trousers were so tight that Julia wondered if he could safely sit down. His maroon coat also fit very snugly, but it was his collar points that fascinated Julia most, for they were so high that Julia wondered how he could turn his head. She looked at him in wonderment, which he unfortunately took to be appreciation of his appearance.

"This is my nephew, Mr. Hazelton-Smythe," Lady Ffoulkes said. "Julia, here, is the oldest," she told him, "and Phoebe is her younger sister."

Julia smiled politely, but Mr. Hazelton-Smythe pulled out his quizzing-glass and began to look her over very carefully.

Julia became embarrassed, then angry as his inspection continued. She looked over to Lady Ffoulkes for some suggestion as to how she should handle such impertinence. Lady Ffoulkes, however, was not as shocked as Julia expected her to be. Apparently she found nothing strange in her nephew's behavior, for she was watching him fondly.

"Harold is looking for a wife," she told Julia. "He has so much to offer, I'm surprised that he hasn't been snatched up already."

Harold smiled indulgently at his aunt and continued to look Julia over.

A quiet cough from behind her reminded Lady Ffoulkes of the other gentleman present. "Oh, yes," she said. "This is Mrs. Sigsby's son, Cecil. Mr. Sigsby to you girls." Pulling Phoebe forward slightly, she said, "This is Phoebe, Cecil."

Mr. Sigsby nodded nervously to the floor, then

stepped back as if he was hoping to blend into the background. Since he was dressed in pale green and gray, it was all too easy to forget his presence.

Further conversation was delayed, for dinner was then announced. Julia was glad of the excuse to move, since Mr. Hazelton-Smythe seemed likely to continue staring as long as time permitted.

"My aunt tells me that you don't have much of a dowry," Mr. Hazelton-Smythe said. He was sitting next to Julia at the table and had remained quiet through two courses and one remove.

Julia tried to look haughty so as to discourage such conversation, but he didn't seem to notice.

"Your dowry?" he repeated patiently.

"Small," she whispered. "Very small. Almost not even there." She smiled what she hoped was a pathetic smile.

"It doesn't really matter," he told her generously. "I have quite enough money of my own." He turned back to his slice of beef and ate it with great relish.

Julia hoped his conversation would end there, but once that dish was removed, he began again.

"Do you have a title?" he asked.

"No." She continued eating.

"It's a pity, but not really your fault, I imagine," he said, once again forgiving her. He looked with interest at the vegetable dishes that had been brought to him.

"Do you speak French?" he asked a while later, refusing some sweetmeats.

"No," lied Julia, although it had been one of her best subjects at school.

"Splendid!" Mr. Hazelton-Smythe congratulated her, much to her surprise. "I think it's terrible the way everyone speaks the language of a country we are at war with. It's quite refreshing to find someone else who refuses to learn their language."

Julia forced herself to smile politely but was really quite puzzled. Nothing seemed to discourage him!

She looked across the table to where Phoebe sat between Mrs. Sigsby and her son. Mrs. Sigsby was talking quite loudly to Lady Ffoulkes so as to leave Phoebe and Cecil free to talk. Cecil, however, had his face practically touching his plate, so he would not have to speak with her. Phoebe caught her sister's eye and smiled at her. She was not too disturbed by the men Lady Ffoulkes had produced for them.

"Do you know how to run a household?" Mr. Hazelton-Smythe asked, interrupting Julia's thoughts.

Julia shook her head. "My sister and I spent most of our time at a boarding school," she told him. "We were so seldom at my grandfather's house that I'm not even sure what keeping house entails." She gave a little laugh that was supposed to indicate that she was rather foolish and helpless.

"That was wise of your grandfather," Mr. Hazelton-Smythe nodded. "No experience means no bad habits to unlearn. All the better to be trained the way your husband wants things done."

It seemed that incompetence was a desired asset, Julia thought sadly. She was quite relieved when Lady Ffoulkes called the girls out of the room, leaving the men with their port.

The guests began arriving soon after dinner was finished, and Julia and Phoebe were caught up in the rush of welcoming everyone. Lady Ffoulkes had only invited a small group of people, saying that if the girls met a few important people, they would be invited places where they could meet many others.

After most of the guests had arrived, Lady Ffoulkes sent the girls off to mingle with them. Most of the people were old friends of Lady Ffoulkes's whom she had not seen since she had returned from India with Sir Giles. They were quite happy to see her and were very sympathetic about her misfortune of having been left with the two girls.

Julia especially felt the disapproval of Lady Ruskin, who was dressed with such elegance that Julia thought she must be a leader in society. Lady Ruskin had promised to secure some invitations for them to some of the more important social events that were left, so "poor Primrose" could be rid of her burden as soon as possible.

More important than the invitations that she promised, in Lady Ffoulkes's eyes, was that she had persuaded her son, Lord Ruskin, to accompany her. Lord Ruskin was tall, quite handsome, and seemed to expect everyone's adoration. He was dressed elegantly in a formal black coat and breeches, with a waistcoat of bright blue. He was very pleasant to the girls, although he seemed a bit more interested in Phoebe's conversation than Julia's. Even so, Julia was surprised when Lady Ffoulkes called her over, leaving Lord Ruskin and Phoebe sitting together.

"I never expected to get him here," Lady Ffoulkes gloated quietly to Julia as she sat down next to her. "He's very popular."

Julia watched him talking to Phoebe. "He seems very nice," she said.

"Nice!" Lady Ffoulkes said in disgust. "Is that all you can say about one of the leaders of fashion and society and one of the richest titles around? I never dreamed that either one of you would make such a match."

"But he's only spoken to us for a few minutes," Julia protested. "What makes you think he is being anything but polite?"

"He didn't have to come," Lady Ffoulkes pointed out. "And he has been speaking with Phoebe far longer than necessary."

"He could hardly just get up and walk away from her," Julia said. "It would be very rude."

"That wouldn't stop him," Lady Ffoulkes shrugged. "He makes his own rules." She watched Phoebe and Lord Ruskin for a few minutes in silence. "I knew he would choose a blonde for his bride because blondes are all the rage now. But you mustn't feel bad," she consoled Julia. "No matter how lovely you look, you are still a brunette, and someone so high in the fashionable world would have to choose what is in style."

"I thought you said he made his own rules," Julia reminded her, disgusted by the conversation.

But Lady Ffoulkes ignored her and went on happily watching them.

Julia could not see what was so special about Lord Ruskin. He was handsome, she acknowledged, but, looking over to where Marc was sitting, noticed that Marc was just as handsome. Marc was also easier to talk to than Lord Ruskin because he didn't have such an exalted opinion of himself. She sighed as Marc greeted a dark-haired young lady who sat down near him and wondered why she had never noticed before just how handsome he was.

"Oh, I think he's leaving," Lady Ffoulkes said.

Lord Ruskin had stood up and was leading Phoebe over to the group of young people sitting at one end of the room.

"I guess he wasn't as taken with Phoebe as you had hoped," Julia said, with a certain amount of relief.

Lady Ffoulkes did not agree, though. "I never hoped that he would stay more than a few minutes," she said. "He's much too popular to spend the whole evening at one event."

Julia thought it must be tiring to be so popular, but kept it to herself since Lord Ruskin was approaching the two of them.

"I must thank you for a most enjoyable evening," he told Lady Ffoulkes politely. "Your wards are quite delightful." Lady Ffoulkes made some unintelligible response. Apparently she was not immune to the famous Ruskin charm. "I hope you will excuse me," he continued, "but I have another engagement." He bowed and left.

"Never thought I'd see him make such a fuss over a chit," Lady Ffoulkes said as she watched him leave the room. "I may be able to abandon Cecil." She saw Julia's confused look, and explained, "If Phoebe can't get an offer on her own, I know that Cecil will take her. I'd rather have her marry Lord Ruskin, though," she admitted.

"What a feather in my cap that would be!" She smiled happily at the thought, then suddenly noticed Julia still at her side. "You can't sit here all night, girl. Get over there where the young men are and get yourself an offer."

Marc was talking to his cousin Claudia Haywood, a tall, fair-haired girl that Julia did not recognize at first. Phoebe was reminding her of the things that they had done together as children, but Claudia seemed to be trying to change the subject. Julia hid a smile as she sat down near them. Claudia may have become quite attractive to the eye, but she was still the same fussy, prim girl that she used to be.

"We haven't seen much of you," Marc laughed as Julia sat down. "We thought you had decided to join the dowagers in glaring at us."

"Hush," Julia warned, "they'll hear you."

Lt. Lyndon came in and apologized for being late. "No real excuse, though," he admitted. "Just took too much time polishing my buttons."

Marc started to tease him, and Muffin interrupted his adoration of Phoebe to laugh. Claudia, however, just glared coolly at him and tried to engage Marc in a private conversation. Julia alone rushed to his defense.

"He has to keep his uniform looking good," she said.

The lieutenant grinned good-naturedly. "Makes you wish you were in uniform, too, doesn't it?"

he asked Marc and Muffin, who only laughed some more.

"You shouldn't laugh at someone who is defending his country," Julia scolded all of them. "He is risking his life." She looked over at the lieutenant. "Have you been in many battles?" she asked. "Have you ever been wounded?"

"He hasn't even been over to France yet," Muffin said, and Lt. Lyndon looked embarrassed.

"I was enjoying being the hero," he complained with a smile.

"Then you weren't ever wounded?" Julia was disappointed.

"No," the lieutenant admitted. "Marc, here, is the only one that has had that honor."

Julia turned toward Marc with new respect in her eyes. "I never knew you were wounded," she whispered in awe. "You should have let me know." She was busy picturing herself leaving school and going to the peninsula to nurse him back to health.

"What battle were you in?" she asked respectfully, giving Muffin and Lt. Lyndon a disapproving look, for they had begun laughing.

"It wasn't exactly a battle," Marc hesitated.

"How did you get wounded, then?" Phoebe asked.

"He was carrying a load of wine bottles for the general and his horse threw him," Lt. Lyndon told them.

"Then he was shot?" Claudia asked.

"No, he landed on the bottles," Muffin laughed.

"But how was he wounded?" Julia did not understand why the men were laughing so. Suddenly an idea occurred to her. "You mean the bottles broke?" she asked.

Muffin nodded. "Into rather sharp pieces."

"Was it that serious?" Phoebe asked.

"Only when he had to sit on his horse," Lt. Lyndon added.

Julia started to laugh. All of her awe for the wounded, heroic Marc was gone. "Oh, Marc," she said. "Was it French wine?"

The others laughed at Marc's expense as Marc stood up testily. "I'm sorry I wasn't there long enough to give some Frenchman a chance to shoot me," he said angrily. "I'm sure they would have been only too happy to oblige you all." He walked away from the group and sat down near Sir Giles.

"Oh, dear," Julia sobered up quickly. "I've offended him. I didn't realize that he would get angry."

"He'll get over it," the lieutenant said.

But Julia was very ashamed of herself. She hadn't meant to hurt Marc's feelings.

The others were talking about a visit to the theater, so Julia quietly left the group and went over to where Marc was sitting. He was talking with Sir Giles and a Mr. Ashton. Julia could hardly interrupt him. Neither could she stand there waiting for a chance to speak to him, for she was receiving disapproving looks from Lady Ruskin. She heard a voice behind her.

"Miss Henley, I've been waiting to speak to you for some time now."

Julia turned dejectedly, for she had forgotten all about Hovering Harold. She tried to look politely interested.

"Why don't we sit over here?" He indicated a settee that was somewhat isolated. She nodded without much enthusiasm and led him over to the seat.

"Do you ride?" Mr. Hazelton-Smythe asked her.

Julia was surprised by the impersonal nature of his question. "Yes," she admitted. "Lady Ffoulkes even arranged for our mares to be brought to London."

He waved aside that bit of information. "Have you ever ridden for a long period?" he continued.

Julia was puzzled. "For a few hours, on a couple of occasions. Never all day."

"Did it exhaust you?"

"No." Where was all this leading? "Why?"

"I've read," he confided to her, "that if a woman is strong enough to ride for several hours without tiring much that she should be able to bear children well. You appear to be fairly strong," he said with obvious approval.

Julia was so shocked she was speechless for a moment. She put her hands up to her cheeks to try to hide the blush that she knew was spreading over her face. "You have no right to ask me such things," she finally managed to say.

"Of course I do," he interrupted, totally unaware of her embarrassment. "I have the right to know what kind of woman I am marrying."

"But you aren't marrying me," she hissed at him, not wanting to call attention to them.

"That depends on what Aunt Primrose and I decide," he said. "When we have reached a decision we will let you know."

"You are extremely rude," Julia said, hoping he would take offense and leave. Suddenly she noticed that it was Marc who seemed to be leaving. She rose quickly. "Excuse me," she said to Mr. Hazelton-Smythe as she hurried after Marc.

"Are you leaving already?" she asked Marc, for he was quite obviously saying good-bye to Lady Ffoulkes.

"I don't usually say good-bye to my hostess unless I am," he said caustically.

"Marc . . ." she began, but he was not waiting around to let her finish.

"I hope your stay in London is pleasant, Julia," he said, and turned away from her.

"I say, Miss Henley," Julia heard Harold behind her. He had taken her arm, so she could not follow Marc into the hallway without causing a scene. "I really do not approve of such rudeness," Harold was telling her quietly. "Now come back here so we can continue our little talk."

He led her back to where they had been sitting, while Julia wondered why she had been in such a hurry to leave school.

Julia was sitting in Phoebe's room several hours later, while her sister brushed her hair and prepared for bed.

"I thought it was a lovely party," Phoebe insisted, not able to understand why Julia was so downcast. "We met a lot of very nice people."

"Some of them were nice," Julia corrected her. "I don't think you could call Mr. Hazelton-Smythe very nice, Or Mr. Sigsby, either," she added.

"I didn't talk much to either of them, so I don't know," Phoebe said, not upset by Julia's gloom.

"Well, you can believe me that Mr. Hazelton-Smythe, or Horrid Harold," she smiled as Phoebe giggled, "is not worth knowing. I don't know why, but he thinks he may decide to marry me." Julia tried to talk very pompously, the way he did.

Phoebe laughed. "Will you?"

"Oh, no." Julia looked quite astonished. "He's insufferable. I'd have to be quite desperate to accept him." Julia stopped, wondering if it might get to that point. No, she assured herself, she would rather seek employment than marry him. But would Lady Ffoulkes see her point of view?

63

"What do you think of Muffin?" Phoebe asked, turning a telling shade of pink.

Julia looked at her in surprise. "I thought you were going to ask me what I thought of Lord Ruskin?"

"Lord Ruskin?" Phoebe was as surprised as Julia had been. "Why would I want to know what you think of him?" She paused for a moment, then asked, "Oh, Julia, you haven't developed a tendre for him, have you? He's awfully high in the instep."

"Not me," Julia laughed. "Lady Ffoulkes has decided that he's developing an interest in you. You see, your coloring is in fashion, while mine, sadly enough, is not." Julia tried to sound miserable, but Phoebe laughed, very much relieved.

"He thinks about himself so much he has no time to develop an interest in anyone else. But you haven't answered my question," Phoebe protested. "Do you like Muffin?"

"He seems very nice," Julia said.

"But he won't speak to me," Phoebe sighed. "He spoke to everyone else, but when I talked to him, he turned a bright red and just smiled. Maybe he didn't like me," she added sadly.

"I think he liked you too much," Julia said, laughing. "He kept watching you like you were a goddess."

Phoebe blushed. "I would like to talk to him, though." She put her brush down, took off her dressing gown, and climbed into bed. "I didn't know that Marc had been wounded," she laughed suddenly. "But I'm not surprised that he didn't mention it."

"I think we hurt his feelings," Julia said quietly.

"Marc's not that sensitive," Phoebe insisted.

"He left early," Julia reminded her.

"So did Lord Ruskin," Phoebe said dryly. "Oh, he probably just had somewhere else to go, Julia. Don't get so worried about it. Or, maybe," she teased, "he was jealous of Handsome Harold."

"It wasn't my fault he was following me around," Julia protested. "I would rather have been with Marc."

"If you have such a preference for Marc's company," Phoebe yawned, "you should have accepted his proposal." She settled down, obviously ready for sleep.

Julia took the hint and went back to her own room, but she couldn't get Phoebe's words out of her mind. Had she been too hasty in refusing Marc?

CHAPTER FOUR

"Julia!" Lady Ffoulkes admonished her as she entered the drawing room the next morning. "Harold will be here soon and you aren't dressed to go driving in the park."

"I wasn't aware I had been invited," Julia said.

"That's because Harold asked my permission," Lady Ffoulkes told her. "Now go and change into that yellow muslin. Harold likes yellow."

Julia went back to her room, quite prepared to wear anything but the yellow muslin. She realized, however, that Lady Ffoulkes was quite likely to send her back up to change again if she did not have it on.

"That's so much better," Lady Ffoulkes said approvingly, when Julia returned. "She did want to look her best for you," she told Mr. Hazelton-Smythe warmly. "When she heard you liked yellow, she went right up to change."

Mr. Hazelton-Smythe smiled condescendingly

at Julia. "Shall we go?" he asked her. "I don't like to keep my horses waiting."

Julia was used to such remarks, for Marc often berated her for keeping his horses waiting. Marc had such glorious horses that he often had trouble keeping them still if she was not ready. Thinking of Marc reminded her of Phoebe's remark the night before. Was Phoebe right? Had she been too hasty in refusing Marc's proposal? Julia sighed as Mr. Hazelton-Smythe handed her up into his curricle.

"You mustn't be afraid," he told her, misinterpreting her sigh. "I am well able to handle these horses."

Julia looked down at his horses. They were a matched pair of bays that looked about fifty years old. Neither of them showed any inclination to move, even when he urged them forward. Julia hid her laughter by pretending to be interested in the homes they were slowly passing. She asked as many questions about them as she could, hoping to keep their conversation on an impersonal level.

They soon reached Hyde Park, which Julia thought was very pretty, but she was disappointed that there were so few other carriages there.

"Most people come in the late afternoon," her companion told her, "but I thought we would have more chance to talk if we came now."

Julia did not know what to say, since she would have welcomed the distractions.

"I have a list here," Mr. Hazelton-Smythe told her as he pulled a piece of paper from the inside of his coat and handed it to her. "It's a list of some of the more influential people in society," he explained. "I wondered how many of them you would have access to."

Julia took the list and glanced quickly at the names. "I'm afraid I don't know any of these people," she told him.

"Oh, not personally, I realize," he acknowledged. "But you must know a daughter or niece of some of them. Take another look at it," he urged as she tried to return it to him. "It would be an excellent way to further my place in society."

Julia would have liked to throw his list at him, or feed it to his horses, but he probably had another copy in his coat. She glanced at the list again, not surprised to see that it contained the names of all the leaders of fashionable society. "No, I don't know any of them," she repeated as she gave the list back to him. "I'm afraid I would not be able to help you meet them."

"Keep the list," he told her. "I'm sure that there must be at least one or two people on it with whom you could find a connection. You can study it at your leisure." They completed a slow circuit of the park before he spoke again. "Many of the older members of society must have heard of your grandfather. Was he active in society?"

"I don't know," Julia admitted reluctantly.

"After my grandmother died eighteen years ago, he retired from society. I have no idea how active he was before that time."

Mr. Hazelton-Smythe just nodded slowly. "It shouldn't be too difficult to find out who his close acquaintances were. Then we can make sure that you are introduced to them as his granddaughter." He smiled confidently to himself. "Yes, that should work out quite well."

"Why should I want to meet his old friends?" Julia asked suspiciously. "I didn't even know my grandfather well."

"That doesn't matter," Mr. Hazelton-Smythe insisted. "Your name will be all that is needed for me to gain admittance into some of the more select groups of society."

"For you?" Julia was astonished. "How will it help you?"

"As your husband, naturally I will be welcome wherever you are welcome," he informed her.

"But you aren't my husband," Julia protested.

"Not yet, I realize," he admitted. "But that can be changed very quickly. Yes, the more I think about it, the more I like the idea," he said almost to himself. "It should work out very well." He turned the horses in the direction of Bolton Street.

"No, it won't work out well," Julia told him angrily. "I have no desire to marry you. I find you quite insufferable." She wished that she knew where they were, so she could jump down and

69

walk home. But, no doubt, she would fall and look like a fool, or get lost. She had to content herself with crossing her arms in defiance and refusing to look at him.

Mr. Hazelton-Smythe was not dismayed. He patted her gloved hand gently. "Now, now, my dear, a little maidenly reticence is fine, but you must learn to moderate it slightly. You wouldn't want to call undue attention to yourself." He smiled calmly. "Aunt Primrose will be so pleased."

Julia was getting quite frightened. Surely Lady Ffoulkes would not force her to marry this insufferable fool, but Julia knew that she could do just that, especially since she had no other likely prospects.

Rather than watch Mr. Hazelton-Smythe manage his horses, Julia maintained a frigid silence and watched the people that they were passing. As they rounded a corner, she caught sight of a familiar face. Riding down the street toward her was Sir Tristan! Julia smiled at him, but she was disappointed that he just rode by.

"I cannot stay any longer right now," Mr. Hazelton-Smythe said as they alighted from his curricle at the house. "But I shall call on Sir Giles later today." He walked up to the house with her, then took his leave.

Julia was barely in the door when Lady Ffoulkes came bustling out of the drawing room. "We have guests," she told Julia. "Go tidy yourself, then come back down." She watched Julia hurry upstairs for a moment, then returned to their guests.

When Julia entered the drawing room a few minutes later, she found Lady Ffoulkes talking with Marc and Muffin, while Lord Ruskin was visiting with Phoebe.

"Ah, Julia," Lady Ffoulkes said. "Come over and join your friends."

Julia greeted them both, but noticed that Marc was rather quiet.

"Why don't you show them the garden?" Lady Ffoulkes suggested, opening the French doors at the end of the room that led out into it.

Julia was surprised by the suggestion, since the garden was small and had not yet been renovated by Sir Giles. She realized, however, that Lady Ffoulkes just wanted her to keep the others occupied while Phoebe entranced Lord Ruskin.

With a sigh Julia led Marc and Muffin into the garden. They walked along the one path that wove among the neglected rosebushes. No one said much, meaning either they were absorbing the beauty of nature, which Julia doubted, or they were hoping to get the tour over with as quickly as possible.

Julia looked over at Marc occasionally as they walked along, but he seemed to be avoiding her. She sighed, thinking of Mr. Hazelton-Smythe. How she wished she had given Marc's proposal more consideration! She certainly wasn't in love with him, but if she had to marry someone, she'd rather it was Marc than anyone else she had met. Phoebe was right! she decided. She had been too hasty. Julia looked over at Marc as they approached the doors to the house and wondered if it really was too late.

Muffin sat down on a bench where he could look into the room and watch Phoebe. He seemed to have forgotten that Marc and Julia were even there. It was a perfect opportunity, and Julia was determined not to waste it.

"Could we talk?" she asked Marc quietly.

Marc looked surprised, but nodded. They moved over to a bench a little distance from the house.

After Marc sat down, Julia began rather hesitantly. "I wanted to apologize about yesterday," she began. "I didn't mean to hurt your feelings."

Marc just shrugged. He had actually given the incident little thought. It had only proved once again that Julia did not appreciate him.

She took a deep breath, and then continued. "I really wanted to tell you that I've changed my mind," she said quickly before she lost her courage. "I've decided that I'll marry you after all."

Marc fought down the sudden surge of excitement that rose within him. "I see," he said. "You have suddenly discovered that you are madly in love with me and can't bear to be parted from me any longer."

Julia was too honest to pretend that her feelings had changed. "No, that's not quite it. It's because of Lady Ffoulkes," she said. "She doesn't want to be responsible for us. Not that I blame her," she added hastily. "She doesn't know us, and we aren't even related very closely. We're only here for the season because she feels the best way to be rid of Phoebe and me would be to find husbands for us."

"And you volunteered my name?" he asked.

"No," Julia said. "I didn't even mention you. It's just that Lady Ffoulkes has given us a month to become engaged. We have to find someone or she'll do it for us. She wants me to marry Mr. Hazelton-Smythe."

Marc looked blank, as if the name meant nothing to him.

"He's her nephew," Julia explained. "He was here last night. He's very determined, and I'm sure that once he approaches Sir Giles about the marriage, I won't be allowed to use the rest of the month to make a decision. I'd be married to him by the end of the week," she said bitterly.

Marc looked at Julia in surprise. He had had no idea that she was being pressured into marriage. He felt like sweeping her into his arms and telling her not to worry, but something held him back. It wasn't that he did not care about her any longer, for his love grew each time that he saw her. It was just a stubborn desire on his part for her to come to him in love. He wanted her to love and need him the way he loved and needed her, not just because she preferred him to Mr. Hazelton-Smythe.

"So," Julia continued bleakly, "I thought if you still wanted to marry me, I would like to marry you." So far he had said very little, Julia thought, which did not seem like a good sign to her. For surely if he cared about her, he would have shown it by this time.

Marc was unsure what to do. He was determined to make Julia appreciate him more. Maybe I've been too available, he thought. If she is no longer sure of me, then she'll realize just how much she does care.

Marc stood up, his decision made. "I'm terribly sorry, Julia," he began, but she looked so crushed that he had to turn away from her. "I'm afraid I can't marry you."

Julia was on her feet in a flash. "What do you mean you can't marry me?" she asked him furiously. Marc was suddenly aware that Muffin was staring at them, so he pulled Julia back down on the bench, but she had more to say.

"You were the one who asked me, you know," she whispered angrily. "You can't just change your mind like that. A gentleman can't do that."

"I did ask you," Marc admitted, "and you answered me. You didn't ask for more time, you just said no. This time you asked me, and I'm under no obligation to say yes any more than you were when I asked you."

"That doesn't make sense," she pouted, close to tears. "You're still angry about last night." Her eyes filled with tears. "I truly am sorry for laughing at you," she said in a voice that shook.

Marc saw the tears and heard the quiver and almost changed his mind. But no, she has to learn to appreciate me. I will marry her, he promised himself, but not yet. "I'm not doing it because I'm angry," he told her, getting another idea. "You told me to find someone else and I have."

"But that was only a week ago," she said in amazement. "How could you have found someone else already?"

"I didn't want to waste any time," he said weakly.

"You must have gone right out after you left me, to look for her," Julia accused him. "And you said you loved me. What kind of love is it that disappears immediately?" She closed her eyes, determined to calm down. "Well," she said more quietly. "I do not intend to marry Mr. Hazelton-Smythe. If you won't marry me, I shall have to find someone else who will. I won't keep you here any longer," she said as she stood up. "I'm sure that we both have other things to do."

They went back into the sitting room, bringing Muffin along with them. Lord Ruskin was taking his leave, so Marc and Muffin did likewise.

Marc thought how well things had gone with Julia as he walked down the few steps to the street. She certainly was not indifferent to him by the time he had left. If the look on her face was any indication, she would have quite cheerfully seen him strung up on Tyburn-tree. He laughed quietly as he thought of her trying to lure some man into marriage. Quiet little schoolgirl Julia. He would have to find some way of preventing Mr. Hazelton-Smythe from talking to Sir Giles, but that shouldn't be too difficult. Once that was done, it was just a matter of time before Julia realized his true worth, and he agreed to marry her.

Marc looked up just in time to see a curricle pull up in front of Sir Giles's townhouse.

"Mr. Hazelton-Smythe!" Marc called out happily, as he climbed up into the curricle next to the very astonished driver. "You are just the man I was hoping to see."

Julia expected momentarily to be informed of her betrothal to Mr. Hazelton-Smythe, but no one mentioned it. By that evening she was so on edge that she continually paced up and down the small sitting room that the girls used. She was restless, jumping at every sound and snapping at Phoebe who responded by bursting into tears.

"Oh, I'm sorry, Phoebe," Julia said, and promptly burst into tears herself. This so astonished her sister that she stopped crying.

"What's wrong, Julia?" she asked. "You haven't been yourself all day." She waited as Julia's tears subsided. "You behaved very strangely with Muffin and Marc this morning."

Julia had been ready to pour out her trouble concerning Mr. Hazelton-Smythe, but at the mention of Marc's name, she began to sob even harder. "Marc doesn't love me anymore," she finally said.

"Why should that upset you?" Phoebe asked. "You always were complaining about the attention he paid you. You ought to be relieved that he won't be pestering you anymore. Oh, for heaven's sake, Julia! Don't start again!" For Julia's tears had begun anew.

"I hate Harold," Julia said vehemently, much to Phoebe's confusion. "I wish he'd fall in a deep hole and never be heard from again."

"I thought we were talking about Marc," Phoebe said. "What has Harold to do with all this?"

"He's decided that he probably will marry me," Julia said with a shudder. "He thinks that grandfather's name may open all sorts of social doors that have been closed to him. He's impossible!"

"That doesn't really seem to be all that serious," Phoebe laughed. "When he asks you, all you have to do is refuse. You still have three weeks left before the season is over, you know."

"I have told him," Julia insisted.

"Did he propose today?" Phoebe wanted to know.

"Well, not really," Julia admitted. "But he makes me so angry that I spend all my time hissing at him."

"Hissing?" Phoebe found it hard to take any of this seriously.

"Yes, hissing!" Julia didn't think it was funny. "He always says upsetting things when other people are around, so I have to be quiet." Phoebe nodded in agreement, but her eyes were sparkling with amusement. "He just won't listen to me when I tell him that I won't marry him! I tell him over and over again," Julia complained, "but he just ignores me." She glared at Phoebe's sudden burst of laughter.

"Oh, Julia," she laughed. "That's just what you said about Marc! You must have told me ten times that he just wouldn't listen to your refusals. Now you are crying because he has taken them seriously." She stopped laughing with some difficulty. "I think your real problem is that you care for Marc more than you thought, and you're sorry that you turned him down. I think that you are in love with Marc and have only found out now, when it may be too late."

"That's silly," Julia declared.

"Is it?" Phoebe asked, but Julia refused to discuss it. She pulled a book off the shelf in the corner and sat down, making it obvious that she intended to read, not talk. The book, however, was a collection of sermons and not very engrossing.

Before Julia had a chance to choose another, Lady Ffoulkes burst into the room. She was there to talk about Harold, but not in the way that Julia feared.

"Just what did you say to Harold today?" she demanded of Julia.

"We just talked," she said lamely.

"But what did you talk about?" Lady Ffoulkes insisted. "He hasn't been to see me all day, and I expected him for dinner tonight."

Julia searched back over their conversation of that morning, trying to find repeatable parts of it. "He thought some of grandfather's friends might be interested in meeting me," Julia offered. Lady Ffoulkes nodded. "And he asked if I knew anyone related to a number of well-known people." Lady Ffoulkes nodded again. "But I didn't," Julia added.

"That doesn't explain his absence."

"He said he couldn't come in," Julia reminded her. "He must have had something to do that took him longer than he expected."

"It's not like him to upset me this way," Lady Ffoulkes said. "He usually is more careful." She sat silently for a few minutes, then rose. "I had better not learn that you did anything to alienate his affections," she warned Julia as she left.

The two girls sat silently after the door closed. Phoebe moved over to sit next to Julia. "I'm sorry I laughed, Julia," she said quietly. "I didn't know that she was pushing him so hard."

Julia tried to smile at her, but it was a rather pitiful attempt. "I don't understand why he's so eager to marry me, though," Julia said. "It's not as if I have a lot of money, and I've tried to discourage him every way I can think of." Julia sat, deep in thought for the moment. "What really frightens me, though, is that Sir Giles could agree to his offer for me, and there would be nothing I could do about it. They could force me to marry him."

"You'll just have to use this time that he's gone to find someone else," Phoebe said, trying to cheer her sister up.

Julia laughed. "You make it sound so easy, but I don't think it will be."

"If only someone would come along and rescue us," Phoebe sighed. "The way Sir Tristan did when our coach was stuck."

"He is here," Julia said, suddenly, remembering that she hadn't told her sister about seeing him. "I saw him while I was riding with Mr. Hazelton-Smythe. But he didn't speak," she added, as Phoebe's face lit up with excitement.

"But he's here in town," Phoebe said. "He'll

find a way to be introduced to us, then you'll have someone else to think about besides Mr. Hazelton-Smythe."

"I'm not sure that he even remembered me," Julia warned her sister, but she did think he may have smiled slightly at her as he passed. Before long Julia had herself convinced that she need not fear Harold, for Sir Tristan was far too charming and handsome to let anyone stand in his way.

CHAPTER FIVE

Sir Tristan had spent three days in a fruitless attempt to discover the extent of Julia's wealth. From his man of business he learned that Sir James Henley had inherited a large fortune from his father almost forty years ago. Then he had married Elizabeth Sawyer, a rare woman who combined beauty and intelligence with the vast Sawyer properties, which were rumored to cover several counties.

About Michael Henley, Julia's father, Sir Tristan could learn little. Apparently, soon out of school, he married a local girl. Not long after the marriage Elizabeth died and Sir James retired from society. Michael and his wife must have also lived quietly, since no one remembered ever having met them. They were both killed in a carriage accident when Julia and Phoebe were quite young. The girls inherited everything that they had.

Sir Tristan did some quick figuring, thinking that the girls inherited from their parents and their grandparents. From that he estimated that the girls shared a yearly income of about 30,000 pounds. He felt his estimate was on the low side, since he had not taken into account the fourteen years that their grandfather had spent as a recluse, doing nothing but increasing the size of his fortune. It was not surprising that Sir Tristan was quite cheerful as he walked down Bond Street on Tuesday morning. His luck had definitely changed.

The girls were strolling through town happily. They had gone for final fittings on some dresses and were quite pleased with them. After they left the dressmakers, they went to Pantheon's Bazaar where they spent another hour, and quite a few pounds, on things that caught their fancy. Phoebe brought a piece of beaded trim for a reticule that she was making. Julia bought a length of lavender muslin, which Phoebe deplored, but Julia said it would be light and comfortable when the weather became hotter and insisted on buying it. Phoebe was soon distracted by a pair of black lace gloves, which required all of Julia's powers of persuasion to keep her from buying. Instead, Phoebe bought a glass bowl that was shaped like a swan. Julia was not sure of its purpose, but it was a harmless enough purchase.

They were walking back to the carriage when they heard a voice behind them.

"Good morning, ladies."

The girls turned to see Sir Tristan behind them.

"And where are you two hurrying off to?" he asked. When they told him, he would not hear of them going back home so quickly. "Surely you can allow me a few minutes of your time," he persuaded. The girls gave in easily, and they all returned to the carriage. Sir Tristan instructed the driver to set them down in the park.

"You know," Sir Tristan said as they strolled along a flowered walkway, "I have been looking all over London for you girls. I was sure that you must have been abducted on your way here and had never actually made it."

They laughed, and Phoebe said teasingly, "You must not have looked very hard because we've been here."

"But where have you been?" he demanded. "You haven't been to the theater, or to Vauxhall Gardens, or to any of the parties and balls I've attended, and I only went to them in the hopes of seeing you."

Julia knew that he was teasing, but Phoebe seemed to believe him. "You did? But we couldn't go to those places until we had been introduced to society," she apologized.

Sir Tristan's smile became a trifle forced. It was lucky, he told himself, that it was Julia who had the larger share of the fortune, for Phoebe's naiveté would become tiresome quite quickly.

"How silly of me to have forgotten," he murmured, and turned to Julia. "Have you been properly introduced to society now? Or do I have to wait still longer?"

"We had a small party on Sunday," she told him with a smile. "So we are able to go out now."

"Tonight we're going to the theater," Phoebe rushed to tell him. "And Friday we are going to Lady Ruskin's ball."

"But this is marvelous!" he exclaimed, finding Phoebe's babbling much easier to bear when she said something worth knowing. "It just so happens that I am engaged to go to the theater tonight, and," he added, "to Lady Ruskin's ball on Friday. You must both save me a dance," he said to the girls, but was looking at Julia.

She smiled quite happily. "I'd be delighted to," she told him quietly.

He smiled in a special way that Julia knew was for her alone. She hugged a sudden burst of happiness to herself as Phoebe started talking again.

"Do you always reserve your dances so far in advance?" Phoebe wanted to know.

"Only when I fear that the lady will be so besieged by partners that I won't get near her," he laughed.

"You were right to ask Julia, then," Phoebe confided to him. "Can you imagine? She's already had an offer!" Phoebe thought that Sir Tristan was eminently suitable for Julia and decided to help him realize just what a popular girl she was.

Julia was abruptly brought back to reality. Why did her sister always stray off the acceptable topics of conversation? She knew that Sir Tristan could not be interested in her offers of marriage, but courtesy would force him to make some reply.

Julia had wronged Sir Tristan, though, for this was a topic that interested him very much, and he hoped that Phoebe would continue to be free with her information.

"I knew someone as lovely as she must have many persistent suitors," he said, looking expectantly at Phoebe.

"Oh, she's quite plagued by suitors," Phoebe agreed.

Julia was a bright red by this time and made some comment about a floral display they were passing, but the others took no notice.

"You don't make it sound as if they are meeting with her favor," Sir Tristan said to Phoebe.

"I'm not sure about that," Phoebe hesitated, thinking of Julia's sudden change toward Marc.

He turned to Julia, a little worried. "But you did refuse your offer?" he asked.

"Yes, I did," Julia said, but surely none of this was his business.

"That's good." Noting Julia's puzzled look, he added, "You should always refuse the first offer. Anyone who would ask you so quickly after your arrival does not really care about you. He has some other reason for wanting to marry you."

Julia nodded. It was what she had thought about Mr. Hazelton-Smythe.

"That's just what I said," Phoebe told Sir Tristan. "I knew that he didn't care about Julia. But we don't know what his reason might be."

"I would guess the obvious one," Sir Tristan suggested. "Money."

"But he said he didn't care about money," Julia said, suddenly anxious to discuss it.

"That's what they always say," he told her gently, "but you shouldn't believe it."

They walked on in silence while Julia wondered why Harold would want to marry her for money when she had none. Sir Tristan, meanwhile, was wondering how to rid the scene of this bounder who was trying to steal Julia's fortune from him.

"What did you say his name was?" Sir Tristan asked.

"Mr. Hazelton-Smythe," Phoebe made a face. "He's Lady Ffoulkes's nephew."

"I don't believe that I know him," Sir Tristan murmured. "Is he going to the theater tonight?"

Phoebe shuddered at the thought. "I would have thought so, but Lady Ffoulkes seems to fear that he's taken Julia in dislike and has hidden himself away, so I'm not sure."

"Then let us hope that he stays hidden away," he said as they reached the carriage. He held

Julia's hand a bit longer than necessary when he helped her up, and smiled comfortingly at her as the carriage pulled away.

Julia somehow forgot all about Mr. Hazelton-Smythe.

"Oh, Julia, isn't this exciting?" Phoebe said as the curtain came down after the first act. "It's just like I imagined the theater would be."

Julia had also found the play to be very enjoyable, but at the present time she was more interested in watching the audience than in discussing the first act. Lady Ffoulkes had insisted that they all, Julia, Phoebe, and the Sigsbys, wait for Harold. He did not come and by the time they arrived at the theater and found their box, it was time for the first act to begin.

They had come only to see the main piece, *A School for Scandal*, and so had missed the First, Second, and Third Musics. Julia hoped they would stay for the farce, for she could not understand getting all dressed up to visit the theater and then missing half the show. It was only after they arrived that she realized that seeing the play was only a secondary motive. Most people came to visit with friends and to be seen by those they wished to impress. From the box that Sir Giles rented for the season, Julia could see the entire floor of the theater and most of the other boxes. She looked around with interest.

"I wonder if there are any people we know here," she said to Phoebe, noticing that they were alone in the box with Mr. Sigsby. "Where did Lady Ffoulkes and your mother go?" she asked him.

"To get some lemonade," he whispered hoarsely. "Would you ladies like some also?" he offered.

"That would be nice," Phoebe agreed uncertainly.

Mr. Sigsby nodded, but did not get up immediately. "I can't leave you alone," he explained. "Wouldn't be proper. Mother'd get very angry."

They smiled their understanding when Lt. Lyndon and Muffin entered the box to say hello. They stayed for a few minutes, and took their leave.

"Muffin still won't talk to me," Phoebe said quietly as the two older ladies returned to the box.

"He was talking," Julia protested.

"Not to me," Phoebe insisted.

"I don't understand what could have happened to him," Lady Ffoulkes said, not for the first time, as Mr. Sigsby left to get the girls their drinks. "It isn't like Harold to leave without telling me, especially since he agreed to come to the theater with us."

"Some young men are quite inconsiderate," Mrs. Sigsby sympathized. "I'm so lucky that dear Cecil isn't like that." She leaned over to where Phoebe was sitting. "He's so very dependable, you know."

"Perhaps I should notify the Runners," Lady Ffoulkes continued, not in the mood to hear "dear Cecil's" praises.

"The Runners!" Mrs. Sigsby was shocked. "You mustn't go to that extreme," she begged her friend. "Think of how mortified he would be when he returns."

"If he returns," Lady Ffoulkes said darkly.

"Depend on it," Mrs. Sigsby said as she patted Lady Ffoulkes's hand. "He's off to the races, or a cockfight, or some other gentlemanly pastime and has forgotten about your theater party. He's a young man, after all, and we know how young men are, don't we?" She smiled up at Cecil who had just returned with the lemonade. He turned very red as he realized that his mother had changed places with him. The only vacant spot was next to Phoebe. He sat down on the far edge of the chair.

Julia had grown quite bored with all this talk of Harold. She hoped that he had finally taken her hints seriously.

"Julia, look," Phoebe said to her. "Isn't that Marc over there?"

Julia looked at the box that Phoebe was indicating. Marc was certainly there, along with Mr. and Mrs. Haywood, and Claudia. "He has been spending a lot of time with her lately," Julia noted, wondering if Claudia was one of the girls who had supposedly fallen under Marc's spell.

"Maybe she has taken your place," Phoebe teased.

"Marc did tell me there was someone else," Julia said quietly, not too pleased with the idea. "Do you think it could be Claudia?"

Phoebe looked over at the two of them talking together in the other box. "It could be," she hesitated. "But they are cousins, so it might mean nothing."

Marc was not unaware of their interest in him and Claudia, and leaned a bit closer to her. Julia and Phoebe need not know that there was nothing at all loverlike in their conversation.

"Quite a few people marry their cousins," Julia said mournfully.

"But Julia, he used to hate her," Phoebe reminded her sister. "You must remember how he would tease her when we were children. He couldn't be in love with her now."

"You mustn't be so ungenerous," Julia scolded. "She's grown very lovely. I'm surprised that she isn't surrounded by swarms of suitors."

Suddenly, Lady Ffoulkes leaned between the girls to look down to the floor of the theater. "Is that Harold down there?" she asked excitedly. But the man in question turned to say something to his companion and she could see it wasn't. "Just some silly fop," she said to Mrs. Sigsby as the play began again.

Julia had lost all interest in the play, and

though she tried hard to concentrate, she was conscious the whole time of the couple in the box near them. Was Claudia Marc's new love? She was relieved when the third act was over and she did not have to pretend an interest in the story. She glanced over at the Haywoods' box and was startled to see it was empty.

"Did they leave?" she whispered to Phoebe.

"Not for the evening," Phoebe laughed at her. "Their cloaks are still there."

Lady Ffoulkes announced that she had seen some friends of Harold's and was going to see if they knew of his whereabouts. She and Mrs. Sigsby departed once more.

"I didn't think he had any friends," Julia said rudely.

To her surprise, Mr. Sigsby grinned. "They just belong to Whites also. I doubt that they are in his confidence. Or want to be."

"Aren't you worried about where he might be?" Phoebe asked him.

"No," he shook his head. "Do you think he'd be worried if I was missing? Would he even notice if I was?"

Julia was quite surprised to see this side of Mr. Sigsby. It disappeared again, however, when someone else entered their box.

"Sir Tristan!" Phoebe cried happily. "I thought I had seen you." She introduced him to Mr. Sigsby, who had once more retreated into the background.

Sir Tristan sat down in the seat that Cecil had occupied. "Every time that I tried to get near your box, I was stopped by some acquaintance. If one more person had waylaid me, I was going to challenge him to a duel, for I was determined to say hello to you." Actually he had been waiting for Lady Ffoulkes and Mrs. Sigsby to leave.

"I almost made it here during the last intermission," he teased, "but you looked so busy that I doubt if you would have noticed me had I come."

Phoebe blushed at his reference to Muffin, which relieved Sir Tristan's mind, for it was Phoebe, not Julia, who had an interest in one of those men. "Are you enjoying the play?" he asked them.

"Oh, yes," Phoebe gushed. "I love the theater."

"It's enjoyable enough," Julia admitted. "But a little frightening, too. Can reputations really be ruined by someone's gossip, as they are in the play?"

Sir Tristan wondered if she might have heard rumors about him, but the question seemed to have been asked in all innocence. What an opportunity! he marveled to himself. "Unfortunately," he said sadly, "people often do repeat things that are not true, and do damage others by it." He smiled at her. "But I'm sure that you would judge a person on what he is, rather than on what others say of him."

"I hope so," Julia agreed.

"You just must not believe everything that you read or hear," he advised. "For some rumors that have caused a great deal of harm have been started out of anger or jealousy." He pointed out some nameless fool, momentarily standing by himself. "Take that gentleman, for example," he said, about to malign the poor man. "He was the victim of another's jealousy. He appeared to be favored in his suit for a lady's hand, so a rival spread vicious rumors about him. Because he had the misfortune to be temporarily low in funds, the other man said he was nothing but a fortune hunter and cared only about the lady's money, and not about her. His beloved heard the rumors and doubted his sincerity. So she married another."

"Oh, how sad!" Phoebe sighed, straining forward to catch a better look at the man, who luckily turned his head so his face was no longer visible. "Did he truly love her?" she asked.

"Completely," Sir Tristan assured her. "It just shows how one should never listen to the judgments of others when your own heart contradicts them." He smiled at Julia, hoping she had gotten the message of his little tale, for she was bound to hear something about him. He hoped she would give him the chance to concoct some tale to deceive her.

Sir Tristan stood up as they heard someone approach the box. "Even though I must go, you will remain in my thoughts," he said quietly as he bowed over Julia's hand. He smiled at Phoebe, nodded at Cecil, and then left.

"Isn't he charming?" Phoebe asked Julia.

"I thought you favored Muffin," Julia said.

"Just because I like Muffin, doesn't mean that I can't appreciate Sir Tristan's charm, does it?" she asked irritably. "Anyway, I was thinking of Sir Tristan for you."

"Yes, he is charming," Julia admitted quietly.

Lady Ffoulkes and Mrs. Sigsby returned, but none the wiser about Mr. Hazelton-Smythe's whereabouts.

Soon after they returned, Lord Ruskin stopped by the box to say hello to Phoebe, which pleased Lady Ffoulkes tremendously. He only stayed for a few minutes, but it was enough for Lady Ffoulkes to begin picturing the wedding.

It wasn't until later, when they were leaving the theater and waiting for their carriage, that Marc deigned to notice them. He came over for a few minutes. After asking them politely how they enjoyed the play, he invited the girls to go riding the next morning. He was assured that they would be delighted to, and left.

"You see," Phoebe whispered to Julia once they were settled in the carriage, "he was just being polite to Claudia. I'm sure he would rather have been with you."

Julia nodded and hoped she was right.

CHAPTER SIX

Phoebe was ready to go riding long before Julia the next morning. She had a new rose velvet riding habit that looked just beautiful on her. It was a simple style that relied more on color than on fussiness. She came into Julia's room when she was dressed.

"Aren't you ready yet?" Phoebe asked.

Julia was trying to force her hair into a new style to impress Marc. She had seen it at the theater the night before, but her hair would not stay where she pinned it, so she finally gave up and fixed it back from her face, letting it fall into soft curls.

"It looks nice that way," Phoebe tried to convince her.

Julia's riding habit was apple green and as plain as Phoebe's, but it enhanced her figure and made her appear taller and more graceful. As Julia was tying a green riband in her hair, a maid came up to tell them that their guests had arrived.

Julia went down, ready to dazzle Marc, only to

discover that he had brought Claudia along and was so busy talking to her that he didn't seem to see Julia at all. Slightly miffed, she gave an overly enthusiastic welcome to Lt. Lyndon and Muffin.

As they mounted their horses in front of the house Julia noticed that there was a certain coolness between Claudia and Lt. Lyndon. Claudia seemed to ignore him completely, and, if he spoke to her, she responded coldly. When she pulled her horse up close to Marc and began to talk very happily to him, Lt. Lyndon looked quite puzzled. Julia thought Claudia's manners left a lot to be desired, and asked the lieutenant if he would ride with her, as she did not know the way. Since Marc was going to ignore her, she might as well find someone to talk to. She was not aware, however, of the way Marc was watching her as he rode behind, or of the number of times that Claudia had to repeat what she was saying because of Marc's inattention.

Marc had originally planned to ride through Green Park, which was right across Piccadilly from Bolton Street, but everyone tired of the park very quickly.

"I've seen enough parks since I came to London," Phoebe complained. "Let's go somewhere interesting."

"We could go to Hyde Park," Claudia suggested.

"No more parks," Phoebe pleaded.

Julia agreed with her. "It would be nice to see something else."

"Let's go to the Tower," Phoebe said.

"Oh, no," Claudia was horrified. "We're not dressed for that."

Julia wondered how one should be dressed to visit the Tower and thought of suggesting that they all go home and put their chains on, but saw Marc assuring Claudia that they would do nothing improper, and decided such a joke would not be appreciated.

"There must be somewhere else we could go," Julia turned to Lt. Lyndon. "I'm tired of riding around parks, too. We saw enough trees and grass when we were at school and at home. We came to see London."

He laughed and held his hand up in mock surrender. "You don't have to convince me," he told her. "I'm willing to go sightseeing."

They finally settled for riding through different parts of the city, so they could see, at least from their horses, some of the places they had heard about.

"This is terrible," Claudia complained as they made their way down Fleet Street. "We should have gone home if no one wanted to ride anymore."

Julia thought of pointing out that they were still riding, but she was having second thoughts about the wisdom of their decision. She was quite relieved when they had passed the prison and could see St. Paul's Cathedral ahead of them. "At least Claudia can't complain about seeing a church," Julia whispered to Phoebe.

Phoebe giggled and turned to look at Muffin who was riding slightly behind the girls.

"Has he spoken to you yet?" Julia asked her.

Phoebe turned back to her sister. "Oh, yes," she said. "He wished me a 'good morning.'" She sighed. "I can't seem to get any response from him. Maybe I should fall off my horse," she said as the idea occurred to her.

"I wouldn't," Julia said, looking down at the street below them. There was so much mud and filth that the stones were barely visible. "Of course, if he could bear to be anywhere near you after you had fallen, it would surely prove his devotion."

Phoebe shuddered and looked at her lovely habit. "I think I'll find another way."

They turned north at St. Paul's to return home by a different route. Before too long they passed by an open field that had many brightly colored tents set up in it.

"What is it?" Phoebe asked Lt. Lyndon, fearing that she wouldn't get an answer from him either. But he did not have to, for Julia cried, "It's St. Bartholomew's Fair!"

The girls were quite eager to go, and Claudia was just as firm about its impropriety.

"You and Marc can go home, then," Phoebe

told her angrily. "I'm sure that Muffin and Lieutenant Lyndon will be happy to escort us through the fair." She turned such a wistful face to poor Sir Archibald that he would have agreed to do anything for her.

The lieutenant agreed, in spite of the way Claudia was glaring at him, and the four of them rode over to a place where they could leave their horses. As they dismounted, they were surprised to see that Marc and Claudia had come along. Claudia looked far from happy, but Marc looked equally determined.

It was early in the day for many of the fair's festivities. There were signs announcing *The New Creation of the World* and *The Re-enactment of the Sinking of the Spanish Armada*, two plays that were to be presented in the evening.

"Oh, do you think we could come back for them?" Phoebe asked. She turned her most charming look on Muffin again, but it had no effect.

"No," he said, but then seemed to regret his firmness. "It really wouldn't be proper," he apologized.

"I've heard about that Creation play," Lt. Lyndon laughed. "They turn wild animals loose in the audience."

Phoebe moved closer to Muffin. "Don't people get hurt?" she asked fearfully.

Muffin put her arm through his. "That's why it's best that we don't go," he told her.

Phoebe looked up at him and smiled, while the lieutenant laughed quietly with Julia. "Actually, they stopped letting the animals loose about a hundred years ago."

They walked along the rows of booths and exhibits. Phoebe was staying very close to Muffin, while Marc dragged Claudia close behind Lt. Lyndon and Julia. They soon came to a small tent that had a short, brightly dressed old woman sitting in front of it.

She jumped up as they approached and ran in front of them. "Let Madame Rosa tell your fortunes," she coaxed. "I see your future before me already, such wonderful futures," she added as she noticed Phoebe's interest.

"Oh, could we?" Phoebe asked Muffin.

"She can't really tell the future," Claudia said in disgust. "She probably isn't even a gypsy."

Madame Rosa gave Claudia a malevolent look and turned back to Phoebe. "You come with Madame Rosa," she said, pointing toward her tent. "I will see a good future for you."

Phoebe looked at her sister, "You'll come, too, won't you, Julia?"

Julia nodded, and the two of them followed Madame Rosa into her tent and sat down where she pointed.

Madame Rosa picked up Phoebe's hand and peered at it in the dim light. "You have many admirers," she said slowly, as Phoebe giggled, "but only one loves you truly." Phoebe sobered up a little. "You must search for him," she added as she looked over Phoebe's shoulder at the gentlemen waiting outside. "You must not be fooled by fancy dress or by his size, for the strength of his shoulders does not tell the strength of his love." Phoebe looked quite pleased with her fortune as the gypsy turned to Julia.

She held Julia's hand for a long time without speaking and Julia began to worry. She had not really taken Phoebe's fortune seriously since the things she said were not very definite, but the silence did worry her. Could she see something bad in her future?

"I see many men around you," Madame Rosa whispered hoarsely. "But there is some problem, and the one you love will not be yours at first." Madame Rosa glanced up to see Julia looking rather worried. The gypsy smiled reassuringly. "I see a soldier," she continued, "and an evil man, but love will win in the end." She leaned back feeling that she must have guessed well, since both girls looked so pleased.

"Oh, Claudia," Phoebe said as they came out of the tent. "You must have her tell your fortune. She's very good."

"It's all nonsense," Claudia insisted. "She can't see into the future. She's only guessing."

"It's just for fun, Miss Haywood," Lt. Lyndon tried to make her relax a little.

"Fun!" she cried, giving him an angry stare. "So consorting with filthy gypsies, and risking our reputations because of it, is your idea of fun, is it?" She turned away as if she could no longer bear the sight of him.

No one knew quite what to say after Claudia's outburst, but Phoebe was determined to make her see that she was wrong about Madame Rosa. "She wasn't just guessing," Phoebe insisted. "She knew that Julia was very popular, and even said that a soldier would love her in the end."

Rather than have the desired effect, this announcement sent Claudia hurrying over to Marc's side, where she refused to speak to anyone else.

The girls were soon distracted by a penny pool in which Julia won a brightly colored top. Then Phoebe saw a sign advertising a show in which a girl walked on a rope high above the ground. Phoebe was intrigued, but all the men insisted that it wasn't a proper show for a young lady to see.

"What's so improper about walking on a rope?" Phoebe pouted.

"It's just not the thing," Marc hedged.

But Phoebe was determined. She stopped walking and glared at them. "You're just trying to spoil my fun. Julia," she appealed to her sister, "you'd like to see it, too, wouldn't you?"

Julia was actually very curious about how one could walk on a rope. She looked over at Muffin and Lt. Lyndon who were looking strangely uncomfortable. "I don't really see why we couldn't," she hesitated.

"For heaven's sake," Marc said in exasperation when no one said anything for a few minutes. "You certainly would see why, and a great deal more, if we went in there. You don't really think they wear long dresses to walk on a rope, do you?"

"Oh," was all Phoebe said, while Julia blushed a fiery red. Claudia stopped pouting long enough to deliver another lecture on the impropriety of the place and suggested that they return home. Diplomatically, Lt. Lyndon pointed out a puppet show that was ready to begin.

They watched the puppet show, which Phoebe declared had the loveliest puppets that she had ever seen. Then they went into another tent and saw three tiny old men with long beards who were called, "The World's Oldest Children." There was also a bearded lady and the world's tallest man.

Nearby, they found a man selling gingerbread, so Marc bought them each a slice, while Muffin bought cider from another vendor. They ate the refreshments in the shade of some trees, discussing which part of the fair to see next.

"This used to be a cloth merchant's fair," Marc told Julia as he moved over to sit next to her. "People would come to the church over there to celebrate St. Bartholomew's feast day, and then sell things at the fair. It used to get very wild."

"It seems rather tame now," Julia said, watching the few people who were present.

"That's only because it's early," Marc warned her, suddenly fearful that she had decided to come back later to see the plays. "It gets very crowded later in the day. There even have been riots in which people were killed," he added. Not sure that all that would deter her, he said, "I hope you aren't thinking of coming back here, because it would be a very stupid thing to do."

Julia had never thought of coming back, and didn't know why he should suddenly get so uppity about things.

"I didn't realize that I was in the habit of doing stupid things," she said haughtily. "But if I did want to do something, I certainly would not refrain from doing it because of your advice." She got up and walked over to Lt. Lyndon. She noticed he had been trying to talk to Claudia, but now he was standing by himself looking rather unhappy.

"You look disapproving," she teased. "Are you going to tell everyone we've been here?"

"Heavens no," he laughed. "Why don't we go and see the animal show?"

Phoebe later admitted that she had been very disappointed in the whole fair, but especially in the wild animal show. It had consisted of a mangy camel, several dispirited monkeys, a sleeping lion surrounded by bugs, and a black bear in a cage.

"It wasn't too exciting, was it?" Phoebe asked Julia as they rode back together.

"No," agreed Julia. She looked up to find Marc watching her disapprovingly. She sighed as he turned to Claudia, wondering why he seemed to prefer her company. Maybe it was because Claudia was so dependable. He could be sure that she would always behave properly and never embarrass him.

Julia was glad when they finally reached home. She and Marc did not part on the best of terms, but Julia did not know why.

Later that afternoon, Julia received a lovely basket of flowers. There was no card, but she was sure they were from Marc. It was his way of apologizing for his rudeness at the fair, she decided, or maybe he was telling her that he regretted his refusal to marry her.

Whatever the reason, Julia looked anxiously for him each time they went out, and hoped that he would come to call. But she saw nothing of him. The only caller they did have was Lord Ruskin, who came to take Phoebe for a ride in the park.

Julia felt quite depressed as Lady Ffoulkes chattered on about Lord Ruskin and Phoebe. She felt deserted by Marc, and Sir Tristan, in spite of all his fancy words, seemed to have also forgotten about her.

Friday evening they were invited to a ball that Lady Ruskin was giving. It was the first really important social event that the girls were to attend, and Lady Ffoulkes was quite anxious that they make a good impression.

Phoebe's dress was of white satin. The neckline and the hem were embroidered with small flowers trimmed with real pearls. She wore a string of pearls around her neck and a few single pearls were secured amid her curls.

Lady Ffoulkes spent hours giving her instructions on how to attract Lord Ruskin's attention. They were so detailed that Phoebe almost lost her enthusiasm for the ball. She could flirt, play with her fan, smile shyly, and agree to dance with eligible partners, but not more than once, except for Lord Ruskin whom she was allowed to dance with twice. Phoebe sighed as she wondered how anyone managed to enjoy themselves at these affairs.

Julia was left to dress in peace, without the benefit of Lady Ffoulkes's advice. Since Mr. Hazelton-Smythe had not yet returned, and Julia had no other visible suitors, Julia thought that Lady Ffoulkes was considering marrying her to Mr. Sigsby. Her only instructions for the evening were to try to attract the attention of some eligible man, and to wear her blue dress.

Julia hated the blue dress and wondered why Lady Ffoulkes, who had been so wise in her other choices, had purchased it. It was far too fussy, Julia thought, as she put the pale blue sarcenet gown on. It was trimmed with numerous ribands of the same color, with bows at the shoulders and the waist. A wide band of ruching created a flounce around the bottom, which Julia thought was all the dress needed to make it positively repulsive. Trying to minimize the effect of the dress, Julia wore her single strand of pearls and had the maid dress her hair very simply.

Lady Ruskin lived in a huge house on Grosvenor Square. When Lady Ffoulkes and the girls arrived, there was a long line of carriages ahead of them, and they had to wait almost half an hour before they reached the carpet that had been rolled out to the street for the guests to walk on.

The entrance hall was lit by hundreds of candles, and Julia could see from where they stood that the ballroom was just as brightly lit. Lady Ruskin received them warmly. Lord Ruskin seemed equally pleased to see them, begging Phoebe to save a dance for him. He did not ask her, much to Lady Ffoulkes's disappointment, to open the ball with him.

"This is going to be a real squeeze," Lady Ffoulkes said happily, as they tried to cross the crowded ballroom.

Since the first person Julia recognized was Mr.

Hazelton-Smythe coming toward them, she did not share Lady Ffoulkes's happy anticipation of the evening.

"Well, Harold," Lady Ffoulkes said as her errant nephew approached them. "Where have you been for the past few days?"

"I have been to Brighton, then to Bath, and then to that heap of stones that you call a home in Somerset," he said impatiently.

"Whoever heard of doing all that traveling in the middle of the season," Lady Ffoulkes said in disgust. She smiled suddenly as a wealthy, though rather old, widower came to ask Phoebe to dance. As soon as his back was turned, she glared at Harold again. "What were you doing in all those places, anyway, trying to hire a house for the summer?"

"I was looking for Sir Giles," he informed her curtly. "I was informed that he had gone to Brighton to buy a yacht."

Lady Ffoulkes interrupted with a snort of laughter. "What would Giles do with a yacht?"

Mr. Hazelton-Smythe ignored her and continued. "Not finding him there, I assumed that he had already left for Bath where he was going to rent a house so that you could take the waters." This time he was forced to notice his aunt, for she shrieked piercingly.

"Bath!" she cried. "Do you think I'm some decrepit old woman who needs the waters to restore me?" She quieted down when she saw that the Dowager Duchess of Ardsley was staring at her. Since the duchess could be quite exhausting when singing the praises of Bath, Lady Ffoulkes smiled sweetly at her before returning to Harold. "I am not going to Bath," she whispered tersely.

He shrugged his shoulders and continued. "I stopped at King's Rest, sure that I would find him there, but the staff had no idea where he was or when he might be there. It was a rather fruitless journey, and I hope you don't mind if I try to forget it." He turned to Julia who had been hoping that someone, anyone, would ask her to dance before Mr. Hazelton-Smythe remembered her presence. "We had better find places before they begin the set," he said, and led her out on the dance floor.

Julia already had an idea why Mr. Hazelton-Smythe was looking for Sir Giles, but hoped that his desire to forget the trip would include her also. But he was not averse to discussing his trip with her.

"I cannot believe that it was anything but an honest mistake on your friend's part," Mr. Hazelton-Smythe said to her as the music began. "And it was kind of him to try to help me catch up with Sir Giles, but I do wish he had bothered to check his information before he passed it on."

Julia was quite puzzled, but she suspected that

she was soon going to have a chance to pay him back for his rudeness to her.

"I had wanted to see Sir Giles about the marriage settlement, and I don't like the delay," he said. "But now that I'm back, I shall see him the first thing in the morning."

Julia smiled sweetly at him and waited until they were just about to be parted by the dance. Then she spoke. "But he's gone," she said politely. "He left yesterday."

The dance separated them suddenly, and Mr. Hazelton-Smythe's frustration was quite evident. When he was close to her once more, he whispered curtly, "Where did he go?"

"Somerset," Julia said as they were swept apart once more.

Mr. Hazelton-Smythe was so upset by the news that he was silent as he led Julia back to Lady Ffoulkes. Then he disappeared into the crowd.

"Whatever made him think Giles was in Brighton?" Lady Ffoulkes asked Julia.

"Someone told him," she answered absently, searching the crowd for a friendly face. Phoebe was returned by the widower and claimed by a red-faced corporal. The next set was almost ready to begin when Marc asked Julia to dance.

She was quite glad to see him, but was not sure that he shared her feelings for he did not seem particularly friendly. That might have been caused by the alarming bruise on the side of his face, and the fact that he was holding his left shoulder rather stiffly. Although it took real effort on her part, Julia decided not to mention his appearance, but rather to thank him for the flowers.

"What flowers?" he asked.

"Weren't you the one who sent me the flowers?" Julia asked uncertainly.

Marc shook his head. "Why did you assume they were from me?"

Julia did not want to admit that she had thought he had sent them as an apology or because he had changed his mind about marrying her, so she merely smiled and tried to laugh it off.

Marc must have realized that he had been rather abrupt, for the next time the dance brought him near he apologized. "I'm sorry, Julia. If I had known that you had wanted some flowers, I'd have been glad to send you some."

He changed the subject, then, but Marc couldn't help wondering just who Julia's secret admirer was.

After the dance was over, Julia and Marc went over to sit near Phoebe. As they arrived, Muffin left.

Phoebe sighed as he disappeared in the direction of the card room. "Am I so horrible that he won't ever dance with me?" she complained.

"He's just shy," Marc said.

"How can he be too shy to ask me to dance?"

Phoebe argued. "He's been in town all season. Do you expect me to believe that he's never asked anyone to dance?"

Marc thought for a moment. "Not very often," he said. "But you have to understand, he's in awe of you. He thinks you're too beautiful to bother with someone like him. Of course, he doesn't know you as well as I do," he teased.

Phoebe didn't know whether to be pleased or annoyed. "Well, I don't know why he should be afraid to talk to me," she said.

"He was an only child," Marc said, "born when both his parents were getting old and had just about given up hope that they'd ever have a child. He grew up alone, without the companionship of other children. We met in school, but he rarely had the chance to meet girls on an informal basis. Now he's just plain afraid of you."

"Well, I won't bite him," she said as she spied Lord Ruskin coming toward her.

"That's something you'll have to convince him of," Marc laughed. "Would you like some orgeat?" he asked Julia. She nodded, and he went to get it.

Lt. Lyndon was sitting nearby but was talking to another young lady, so Julia used the time to look at the people just arriving. Suddenly she thought she caught sight of Sir Tristan's fair hair behind some of the other late arrivals. She stood up abruptly to get a better look.

Unfortunately, as she stood up Marc arrived

with her drink, and she bumped into him rather sharply. He spilled most of it on the floor, but Julia barely noticed for she had seen the look of pain on Marc's face and the way he was clutching his shoulder.

"Oh, Marc, is there something wrong?" she cried.

All she received for her concern was an annoyed look as he sat down on the sofa next to her. She noticed that many of the people near them had stopped talking and had turned to see what had happened, so she smiled pleasantly and tried to look as if everything was normal.

"I didn't mean to bump you," she whispered under her breath to him. "I'm terribly sorry."

"Would you stop whispering?" he said angrily. "It looks like you're making an assignation with me!"

"What are you so angry about?" Julia asked. "I didn't bump you hard enough to hurt you."

"It was your fault, anyway," Marc said bitterly, still rubbing his shoulder. "I could use a drink about now," he said, looking around him.

"There's a little orgeat left in the glass," Julia said, offering it to him.

"That wasn't what I had in mind."

Julia sat in silence for a moment, hopefully giving him time to regain his good humor. "Just how did I cause your shoulder to be sore?" she asked. "I haven't even seen you for days."

"No, but you left me with that stupid comment about not listening to my advice," he said. "I assumed by it that you meant to return to the fair that evening and I thought I'd better go also, so I'd be there when you needed help. When I arrived, I saw a dark-haired girl being manhandled by some ruffians. I assumed it was you and went to your rescue. I got these for my trouble." He pointed to his bruises. "The girl didn't thank me either, for the first one that I hit was her young man, and she didn't take kindly to my interference."

"Oh, Marc," Julia shook her head and laughed quietly. "Why would you think that I'd be so foolish as to go back there? I'm not entirely unaware of the restrictions of society."

"It seemed like just the sort of ill-advised escapade you'd embark on," he was stung to reply.

"That's not fair," Julia cried, now completely out of sympathy with him. "You have no reason to believe that I would act so foolishly." She stood up quickly.

"Are you free for this dance, Miss Henley?" Julia found Lt. Lyndon standing in front of her. She glanced at Marc to make sure that he was aware of the invitation, tossed her head defiantly, and went off with the lieutenant.

Julia did not see Marc again for a while. Then she saw him dancing with Lady Annabella, and then with Claudia. All of her former anger was gone. She just felt very hurt, suddenly, and wished she could go home, especially when she saw Mr. Hazelton-Smythe heading toward her. She simply couldn't take him any longer, so she ducked into a hallway where she bumped into yet another gentleman.

Goodness, she said to herself. Was this all she was capable of this evening? Bumping into gentlemen? It was all the fault of this horrid dress, she thought, believing in putting the blame where it belonged. I look like a short little frump, and I'm acting like one. She stepped back to apologize and saw Sir Tristan's amused eyes smiling down at her.

"Fancy meeting you like this," he drawled.

Julia laughed away her embarrassment. "I had hoped to see you, but I hadn't planned on knocking you down to do it."

He put her arm through his and strolled out to the terrace with her. "You looked like you were in flight," he remarked. "Were you being plagued by one of the all too persistent suitors?"

"Yes," Julia admitted. "But there is only one of them. Although, sometimes he does seem more like twenty," she added with a laugh.

"Ah, the nephew," he said. "He must have returned."

Julia nodded, quite surprised at Sir Tristan's memory.

"You must point him out to me," he told her. "I have a strange desire to see what this graceless boor looks like."

Julia agreed and since they could see Mr. Hazelton-Smythe standing near the doors to the terrace, she pointed him out to Sir Tristan.

"He certainly does not look like he should be allowed to bother you," Sir Tristan decided. "Would you like me to arrange his death?" he joked.

"Oh, nothing so drastic," Julia laughed. "If he would just take to wandering about the countryside again, I would be satisfied."

"Does he often wander about the countryside?" he asked in surprise. "He sounds like a candidate for Bedlam. Maybe we should just admit him, instead of murdering him."

Julia smiled. It was good to be in the company of someone so enjoyable.

"Tell me," Sir Tristan said. "Did you get my flowers?"

"Your flowers?" Julia asked in surprise. "They were from you?"

"Of course," he frowned. "I thought you would realize that."

"I . . ." Julia hesitated. "I wasn't sure since there was no card," she tried to explain.

"But it's so much more romantic that way, don't you think?"

"Only if you know who's being romantic," Julia teased. "But they were quite beautiful," she said seriously. "I do thank you for them."

"Oh, come. I think you can thank me better than that," Sir Tristan laughed, and pulled her over into a shadowy section of the terrace. Julia noticed how alone they were out there.

Julia did not object as he bent down to kiss her, for Sir Tristan was very attractive and she was curious to know what it would be like to be kissed by him. But she was disappointed, for his lips seemed cold and lifeless against hers. He, apparently, had found nothing lacking since he seemed loath to move away from her.

"You must forgive me," he said a trifle breathlessly, "but you have bewitched me, and I could no longer deny myself the pleasure of your lips."

Julia smiled at him. She could hardly tell him that to her it had seemed more like kissing a fish than a person. As he led her back inside Julia wondered at her curiously flat feeling. Why couldn't she respond to someone who sincerely cared about her, like Sir Tristan, instead of being annoyed because Marc no longer did?

Julia was quite relieved when Lady Ffoulkes decided it was time to leave. The only good thing about the evening was that Mr. Hazelton-Smythe apparently had left early.

* * *

Mr. Hazelton-Smythe had decided that if he was going to travel into Somerset once more, he would need a good night's rest, so he left the party earlier than most of the other guests. He had planned to leave London the next morning, but found that his plans had been changed for him. He dimly remembered starting to walk across Grosvenor's Square, since he could find no hackneys, and then being jumped by some Mohocks. He awoke to find himself with a sore head.

He looked around him now in aversion. The room he was in was quite unclean. He heard a nauseating sound behind, and slowly turned his head. He beheld a repulsively unkempt man eating a greasy piece of meat. He took huge bites, then wiped his face clean with his sleeve. Mr. Hazelton-Smythe shuddered in horror as the man looked up and saw him.

"So yer awake at last, eh?" He called out to someone beyond the closed door, then gestured to the other chair at the table. "Make yerself at 'ome," he said. "Yer gonna be our guest fer a while."

CHAPTER SEVEN

Early the next week, Lady Ffoulkes was surprised to receive a morning call from Mrs. Haywood and Claudia. It seems that they were planning a trip to Vauxhall Gardens and wanted the girls to accompany them. Lady Ffoulkes agreed quite readily for it was more exposure to young men, and yet she did not have to be bothered with chaperoning them.

"The girls are going shopping this morning, and then to Hookhams. Why don't you stay and go with them?" Lady Ffoulkes said to Claudia, trying to appear sociable. "The coachman can bring her home when they are finished," she assured Mrs. Haywood.

Julia was surprised to find Claudia in the sitting room when she entered it several minutes later. Lady Ffoulkes had already departed, so it was up to Claudia to explain her presence.

"That's nice," Julia said, trying to be enthusiastic when told that Claudia was accompany them.

Claudia herself didn't look very pleased about it. They sat in silence for a few minutes waiting for Phoebe. "Is anything wrong, Claudia?" Julia finally asked, for she seemed to be looking particularly melancholy.

"Oh, no," Claudia assured her, then promptly burst into tears. She cried for a few minutes, then said brokenly, "I know that you don't really care," she sobbed, "but I'm so unhappy." She took a few more minutes to cry.

Julia dug into her reticule to find a handkerchief and handed it to Claudia. "Of course I care," Julia told her. "I don't like to see you so upset."

Claudia wiped her eyes, and Julia wondered briefly how she remained so pretty when she cried, for Julia's face always got red and blotchy. She chided herself for being uncharitable, and said to Claudia, "If it will help to talk about it, then please do. But you don't have to," she added quickly, for she didn't want to force her confidence.

Claudia seemed to have made up her mind to talk, though, for she wiped her eyes again and said, "Maybe if I told you about it, it would help."

Julia did not know exactly how she could help, but assumed that Claudia would feel better just from talking to someone about her problem. Julia nodded, and waited for Claudia to begin.

"You see, it's because of . . . this man," Claudia obviously did not want to mention his name. "We had been very close, at least I thought we had been very close. I might have been wrong." Julia nodded understandingly as Claudia continued. "This was all before you came to London, but he was always asking me to dance and he took me out riding. He seemed to like my company." She paused for a moment to cry some more, while Julia wished impatiently that she would leave out all the dramatics. "I could not be sure if he was going to approach my father with an offer, and I got tired of waiting for him to make up his mind, so I decided to make him jealous. I have known him for a long time, you see, and I feared he might not have any stronger feelings for me than just friendship."

Julia had the horrible suspicion that this nameless gentleman was Marc. That was why Claudia hesitated before telling her all this, but then she must have decided that Julia could help if she knew the truth.

"I started pretending to like other men," Claudia went on, "but he didn't seem to mind. Then he started to pay attention to this other girl, and now he seems to prefer her company. At least he did at Lady Ruskin's ball." She gave way to another burst of tears.

Julia sat in stunned silence. So Marc was in love with Claudia, and had been all along. But why had he proposed to her before she had ever arrived in London?

"Maybe he's just trying to make you jealous," Julia suggested.

"Oh, no, he wouldn't do something like that," Claudia said, shocked that Julia would suspect such things of her beloved. "He's not like that," she insisted. "It's all my fault. I drove him to that other girl, but I can't believe he really cares about her. Not like he cared about me."

"Maybe he feels sorry for her," Julia said. Maybe Marc had felt sorry for her after her grandfather died.

"I suppose he might," Claudia agreed slowly. "But I don't think he realizes how hurt I am by the way he's acting. He thinks that I'm just a hopeless flirt who never really cared about him. I don't know how to get him back," she sobbed.

Julia had a strange desire to join Claudia in her tears, but waited patiently until she finished. "Everything will work out," she tried to assure her. "Perhaps if you were to single him out for attention a bit more, he might realize that your feelings are sincere."

"I can try, I guess," Claudia said doubtfully.

"If he truly cared about you, his feelings wouldn't suddenly change," Julia said, thinking of how she had accused Marc of that. "I'm sure he still loves you. He's only with that other girl out of pity." The more Julia tried to convince Claudia that Marc really loved her, not this other girl, the more Julia herself believed it.

"I guess you may be right," Claudia said, trying to smile. "I feel very foolish now."

"Well, you mustn't," Julia said positively. "I only hope that our talk has helped."

Phoebe entered the room a few minutes later as the girls were innocently discussing a three-quarter-length pelisse, trimmed in fur, that Claudia wanted to buy. Claudia was doing most of the talking, however, for Julia did not have much interest in clothes at the moment. She kept thinking of Marc, and how his love had never been hers.

Julia did not think that she could bear seeing Marc and Claudia together and tried to avoid the trip to Vauxhall Gardens. Every excuse she gave to Lady Ffoulkes was rejected, however, and Tuesday night she was waiting with Phoebe for the Haywoods.

As they boarded the sculls at Westminster, and saw the lights of the garden welcoming them, she was glad she was there. Just because Marc was in love with someone else was no reason that she should not see one of London's most popular attractions.

The Haywoods had reserved a box and the girls were delighted by what they could see from it. Marc, Muffin, and Lt. Lyndon soon joined them, as Julia suspected they would. They all sat watching the crowd for a short while.

"Would you like to dance with me in the

pavilion?" Marc asked. Julia looked up and was quite surprised to find he was talking to her.

"That would be nice," Julia agreed reluctantly, not knowing how to refuse.

Marc opened the door of their box and led her over to the big rotunda where the orchestra was. He made no attempt at conversation, which Julia was quite glad of, since it enabled her to simply enjoy the dance. Julia sighed as it ended, for it had seemed awfully short, and let Marc lead her back to the box.

"Is this the way back?" Julia asked Marc, thinking it seemed much darker than she remembered.

The walk they were on was lit only by occasional lanterns hanging from the trees. The noise from the dancing in the pavilion seemed very far away and Julia had the sense of being alone with Marc in their own separate world. The trees made a canopy over the walkway and increased Julia's sense of isolation.

"I thought we'd go the long way back," Marc whispered, taking her hand and placing it on his arm.

They walked a bit further, and although Julia was glad to feel Marc close to her, she was feeling anything but at peace. Just the feel of his arm under her hand made all her senses tingle, and she was very conscious of his nearness. Suddenly, from around a bend in the path a noisy bunch of party goers appeared, breaking the spell of silence.

Julia pressed closer to Marc to give them room to pass. Marc slipped his arm around her waist and pulled her off the path, under the shadows of the trees.

Julia looked up into his face, dimly conscious that it was quiet again. The faint light from the lanterns flickered through the leaves of the trees, letting her see his face just as his lips came down to meet hers.

As Marc's lips touched hers, she forgot all about his love for Claudia and was aware of only the two of them. Somehow her arms slipped up around his neck to keep him close, while his lips moved to the hollow at the base of her neck.

"Julia," he whispered softly in her ear. She knew that she was trembling beneath his caresses, but had no desire to make him stop.

"Julia," he whispered again as he held her even tighter in his arms, and nibbled at her earlobe. "Marry me, Julia," he said softly. "Tell me you'll marry me."

Julia suddenly remembered Claudia and pulled out of his arms, trying to stop shaking.

"No," she whispered hoarsely. "I can't." She reminded herself that he loved Claudia, wanting nothing more than to be in his arms again. She loved him, she realized with a shock.

"What do you mean you can't?" Marc cried, trying to pull her back into his arms again, but unable to as she moved back onto the path. "You weren't kissing me like I repulsed you."

"Well, I like the way you kiss," she said feebly.

"You like the way I kiss! Since when have you become an expert in kissing?"

The band suddenly could be heard in the distance, reminding them that they were not alone. "Come now, Julia," Marc said more softly. "I don't know what game you're playing but let's end it. We belong together, you and I." He tried again to pull her into his arms, but she broke free from his hold.

"You're the one who's playing some sort of game," Julia told him. "I've always said that I wouldn't marry you. I haven't changed."

"Just a few days ago you were begging me to marry you to keep Lady Ffoulkes from marrying you to her nephew," he reminded her curtly. "So you certainly have changed your mind."

Another couple came strolling down the path. The man was whispering to the woman, who occasionally burst into harsh laughter. Marc cursed beneath his breath, and grabbed Julia's arm. He pulled her a little way down the walk until they reached a smaller path that led away.

Julia and Marc went up the smaller path, at the end of which was a small templelike structure. Under normal circumstances, Julia would have been very curious about the people they had seen and about the small temples that dotted the park, but at the moment she was too upset to even notice them.

She was only aware of these things as diversions that would give her more time to think, for she was quite shaken to learn the reason for Marc's abrupt change of mind. He was offering for her out of pity, as she had suspected. It was her story of Lady Ffoulkes and Harold that had done it, and now he felt it was his duty as an old friend to help her, even if he didn't love her. Once he realized the sincerity of Claudia's feelings, though, he would be quite glad that Julia had not accepted him. Her only problem was how to convince him that she regretted her proposal to him.

"Julia," he whispered urgently. "Why must we constantly fence and argue with one another? Say you'll marry me and put an end to this farce."

"Things have changed since I told you about Lady Ffoulkes," she said slowly.

"Changed in what way?" he asked. "You can't be engaged to Harold, for he's still chasing after Sir Giles."

"No, it's not Harold," she said, knowing suddenly what excuse he would have to accept. "But ... but there is someone else."

Marc had been reaching out for her, but his arms dropped suddenly. "Someone else?" he repeated blankly. "Are you telling me that you've fallen in love?"

"Yes," she whispered, close to tears, for that at least was true. She had fallen in love.

"Who is it?" he asked. "Who have you fallen in love with?"

Julia knew that she could not stand much more of this conversation. She was trying to do what was best for Marc, but she was close to the breaking point. "Oh Marc," she pleaded, "leave me alone." She felt, rather than saw, him reaching out for her, but knew that if she was in his arms once more she would be lost. With an incoherent cry, she pushed past him and ran down the dark path. She had no idea where she was going, just as long as it was away from Marc.

Julia heard Marc call her and knew he was coming after her. She turned onto side paths and pushed through crowds of people. When she could run no longer, she sank onto a bench along the path to catch her breath. After a few minutes she looked around her and realized that she was quite lost. The gardens were very large, and the sections set aside for dancing and for refreshments were a small part of the whole area. She had no idea how to find her way back.

A gentleman suddenly appeared at her side on the bench. "Hello, honey," he said, trying to gain control of her hand. "Have you been waiting for me long?"

She pushed him away fearfully and hurried back

down the path, but she could hear his laughter following her. She began to realize that not only did she have the problem of being lost, but of appearing as prey to any number of strange men.

Two foppishly dressed men approached her as she hesitated at a crossroads, but she did not linger to hear what they had to say. She was getting quite frightened by this time, and scolded herself for running away. There had been no way that Marc could have forced her to marry him, all she would have had to do was remain firm.

She turned a corner abruptly and found herself in the arms of yet another man. She was about to pull herself away when she recognized his voice. "Oh, Sir Tristan," she cried, and leaned against him in relief.

"Miss Henley?" he was quite surprised. "What are you doing out here all alone?" He felt her trembling and was concerned. "Are you all right?"

She nodded, not trusting her voice yet. He pulled her over to a bench before a statue of Venus, and waited for her to regain her composure.

After a moment he repeated his question. "How did you come to be out here alone?" he asked.

"I was separated from my group," she explained, not wanting to go into any more detail. "I got lost and couldn't find my way. There were some men . . ." She began to shiver again and found his arm tightly across her shoulders.

"Did they harm you?" he asked angrily. "Do you know who they were?"

"Oh, no," she said. "I'm sure it was my fault for being out here alone. I have no idea who they were, for I didn't take time to look at them."

He waited a few minutes more, savoring the realization that fate had allowed him once more to come to her rescue. He gave a moment's thought as how to best use that fact. "Do you feel up to returning to your friends now? I would take you home, but I'm sure that they must be worrying."

"Oh, I don't want to go home yet," she cried. "I'd miss the fireworks."

"Then you must be feeling better," he laughed. He stood up and offered her his arm. "Shall we return?"

They walked along in silence for a short way, while Sir Tristan allowed her time to relax and feel at ease in his company.

"I am sorry that you were frightened," he told her. "But I'm not sorry to have this chance to see you again." Encouraged by her smile, he continued. "I was afraid that I might have offended you the last time we met."

Julia had to think back, wondering what he might have done to offend her. With a start she remembered Lady Ruskin's ball. "No, I wasn't offended," she hastened to assure him. How could she have been when she had forgotten all about his kiss?

"I'm so glad," he said quietly. "I feared that you would doubt my sincerity because I let myself be overcome by your nearness. You must know that I have only the highest regard for you." He stopped walking and looked down at her, waiting for some sign of encouragement.

Julia did not know what to say. She knew she ought to be flattered that someone as important as Sir Tristan seemed to be interested in her. But it was all happening too close to her scene with Marc for her to think clearly. She had believed Marc's words, only to learn that she shouldn't have. Now she found herself doubting Sir Tristan's words, which was silly, for hadn't she found that he could be trusted?

Some of her thoughts must have been apparent in her face. "No," Sir Tristan said, placing his fingertips lightly over her mouth. "Don't say anything. I can see that this was not the time for me to speak. You must excuse my impatience this evening. But I shall not wait too much longer."

"Thank you," Julia smiled at him. "It has been a trying day." He was so understanding of her feelings that she felt guilty she did not return his affection.

They walked further along the path, and Julia could see the bright lights and the boxes where people were sitting. "I hadn't realized that I was so close," she laughed in embarrassment.

"You aren't regretting the time we spent together, are you?" Sir Tristan asked, looking quite injured. He was pleased to see her guilty reaction.

"No, no," she said quickly. "I was quite pleased to see you again. It just seemed silly of me to be so worried when I was so close."

Sir Tristan stopped at the edge of the boxes and looked down at her. "You might find it awkward to explain how you came to be in my presence, so I'll leave you here." He picked up her hand and brought it to his lips. "I shall be seeing you again quite soon, I can assure you." He kissed her hand gently, then reluctantly let it go.

Sir Tristan stepped back and watched as Julia walked down the row. As she reached the Haywoods' box she turned and looked at him. He raised his hand slightly, and tried to look lonely. Then she disappeared into the box.

Sir Tristan did not waste any more time standing at the end of the row. He had accomplished his purpose and quite cheerfully went in search of someone a bit less pure, and a lot more willing than Julia. He was sure that Julia and her fortune were almost ready to drop into his lap. He laughed out loud when he thought of how gullible Julia was. She actually had believed all his flummery!

A heavily painted young woman caught his eye

as she leaned against the low wall that edged the path. Her red satin dress was cut low and fit tightly. It left little to his imagination. She looked up at him.

"Were you lookin' fer me, my lord?" she asked in a seductive whisper as she moved slowly over to his side.

He looked at her for a minute, taking in the all too visible signs of her charms. "Yes, I was," he laughed. "I really think I was." He took her arm and led her away from the bright lights.

Julia expected many questions about where she had been, but no one seemed to have noticed that she had been gone. Mr. and Mrs. Haywood were making small talk with Lt. Lyndon and Claudia, but Claudia did not seem to be at ease. Julia decided to entertain the lieutenant to show Claudia that she need not worry since Julia had no interest in Marc.

Phoebe and Muffin returned from the dance floor a few moments before Marc came bursting into the box. He stopped short when he saw Julia sitting there laughing with the lieutenant. Everyone looked up at his unusual entrance, but he sat down without explanation.

Claudia smiled at him and tried to engage him in conversation, but he was looking glum and was not very receptive. Julia suggested that they all take a walk, hoping that it would help Claudia talk to Marc. He seemed anything but enthusiastic about the idea, but eventually gave in.

Julia immediately took Lt. Lyndon's arm and moved slightly away from the rest, while Phoebe walked rather spiritlessly at Muffin's side. Marc and Claudia were left alone. Julia was quite pleased with her maneuver and could only hope that Claudia would make some headway in convincing Marc that she loved him.

Marc was getting rather tired of his cousin, but was even more dejected by the way Julia had taken Lt. Lyndon's arm. Was he the fellow that she had fallen in love with? Lyndon was a good enough fellow, but not right for Julia, and Marc did not think he returned her feelings. Then he saw the lieutenant protectively guide Julia around some rowdy men, and feared he was wrong. Maybe Lyndon had fallen for her, Marc told himself. God knew she was lovely enough to have every man in London in love with her.

As magnificent as the firework display was, no one really enjoyed it. Julia was quite glad when Mr. Haywood said it was time to leave. She didn't think she could have kept up her pretense of having a good time much longer.

CHAPTER EIGHT

Phoebe threw herself down on her sister's bed the next morning. It was quite obvious that she was suffering from a severe fit of the dismals. Since she had been unfailingly optimistic throughout Julia's periods of depression, Julia was anxious to know the cause.

She put down her hairbrush and sat next to her sister. "What's wrong, Phoebe?" she asked.

Phoebe looked as if she had spent the night crying. "It's Muffin," she explained. "I think he hates me."

"Oh, is that all?" Julia laughed and got up again. "How can you say he hates you when he's always watching you so adoringly?"

"Because that's all he does," Phoebe said bitterly. "He just sits and watches me like I'm a statue on display."

"But he danced with you last night," Julia pointed out. "And you were walking together."

"Yes, he danced with me," Phoebe admitted,

"after I forced him into it. Then he kept pointing out other men that he knew, suggesting that I might want him to introduce me, as he was sure that I would rather be dancing with someone like them." Phoebe stood up and went over to the window. "He just would not believe that I might prefer to be with him."

"What about the walk?" Julia asked, fearing the worst.

"Well, he didn't point out anyone he was sure I'd rather be walking with, but neither did he talk very much."

"But he did talk some?" Julia asked hopefully.

"Oh, yes," Phoebe was being sarcastic. "He said, 'Watch your step' and 'Excuse me' when he moved a little closer to me to let some others past." She sat down next to her sister again. "I know that Marc said he's very shy, but I just can't seem to get any response. I really like him, but I don't think that it's any use."

"I think it depends on how much you really like him," Julia said. "Do you mean that you like to do things with him, or that he's the one you want to marry?"

Julia did not really need Phoebe's blush to tell her that her second guess had been right.

"Does it matter what I prefer, though?" Phoebe said. "We have less than two weeks left, and I don't see how I can get him to offer for me."

"The first thing you must do is cheer up," Julia

told her bracingly. "You'll never get him to offer for you if you are moping around. If we both work on it, I'm sure that we can find a way to get around his shyness." She thought for a moment. "Maybe he could rescue you from highwaymen, or better yet, we should let him compromise you, then he'll be forced to marry you."

Julia's suggestions had the desired effect, and soon Phoebe was laughing. "We can try," she told Julia as they made their way to Lady Ffoulkes's room.

Lady Ffoulkes had their day all planned for them. "You're going to visit Mrs. Sigsby this morning," she told them. "Cecil will come for you soon after breakfast, so be ready." She noted Phoebe did not seem too thrilled at the prospect, and reminded her that the season was almost over. "There's very little time left," she said. "I haven't noticed you forming any other attachments elsewhere." She looked wistful for a moment. "I had hopes you might attach Lord Ruskin, but I haven't seen him lately, so you must have done something to disgust him."

Phoebe did not care whether Lord Ruskin sought her out or not, but she did happen to know where he was. "He's gone to Bath to get his hair cut," she told Lady Ffoulkes.

"Bath, for a haircut!" she could not believe her ears.

"He said his favorite barber is there and he must get his hair cut before the prince regent's fete on the nineteenth," Phoebe explained.

"Oh, now I understand," Lady Ffoulkes nodded. "It will be a glorious affair."

Something in her tone of voice made Phoebe look at her in surprise. "Were we invited?"

Lady Ffoulkes nodded. "Lady Ruskin managed to get us invitations. After all, he's inviting close to two thousand people. The three of us will hardly make the numbers awkward." She was silent for a moment, but from the look on her face the girls knew she was working out a plan. "Maybe we could persuade Lord Ruskin to accompany us," she mused quietly. Then she added, looking at Phoebe, "Well, don't get your hopes up. And Cecil will make you a fine husband if Lord Ruskin doesn't make an offer soon." She sighed contentedly. "We should have both you girls settled very soon, for Harold should be back any day now from seeing Giles." She waved the girls out of the room. "Have your breakfast quickly. Mrs. Sigsby does not like to be kept waiting."

Mr. Hazelton-Smythe felt wretched as he awoke, fearing that this day would be no different from the last four. He was still being held in the same filthy room, but he had no idea why. He had seen no one except for Mr. Heggit, the unkempt man, when he brought him food at mealtimes. The first day he had a tendency to linger, but the last few days he brought the food and disappeared.

Mr. Hazelton-Smythe looked up as someone entered the room. It was Mr. Heggit carrying a tray of breakfast. Mr. Hazelton-Smythe's eyes began to water as he came near, for he reeked of onions, garlic, and gin.

"Wake up there, Harry," he called happily. "Got a spot of ale fer ya, and a bite of beef." He put the tray down and grinned as Mr. Hazelton-Smythe refused the food. "Sorry I ain't been 'round much the last few days ta keep ya company, but I never figured to have a fancy swell, like ya, here with me." He eyed his clothes with obvious pleasure. "I always had me a mind to wear one of them necktie things," he admitted.

Mr. Hazelton-Smythe shuddered as he thought of his purely laundered cravats being touched by Mr. Heggit's filthy hands. "Perhaps I'll have a bite to eat, after all," he said, gingerly trying the bread. It wasn't fresh but neither was it noticeably wormy.

"Just why am I here?" he asked, after he had eaten the bread and drank half the ale. Mr. Heggit was still there, so he decided to pump him for information. "I'm afraid I can see no reason for it." He looked about in vain for a napkin.

"I thought ya must know," Mr. Heggit said, scratching his head thoughtfully. "Figured it was some joke. You ain't in no bet fer a lot of money?"

"I do not gamble," Mr. Hazelton-Smythe said, "nor do I race."

Mr. Heggit looked puzzled. "All I was ta do was grab ya, and keep ya here fer a week," he said, rubbing his unshaven chin. "And I was ta get a hundred guineas. His lordship described ya perfect," he added. "Right down ta the gold tassly things on yer boots."

They both looked at the tassels hanging forlornly from Mr. Hazelton-Smythe's boots.

"But he didn't tell me no reason," Mr. Heggit shrugged. "And a century's a century."

"Who's his lordship?" Mr. Hazelton-Smythe asked.

But Mr. Heggit didn't know. "He were dressed like the prince hisself," he claimed.

Someone called Mr. Heggit from below and he rose from his chair. "Don't ya fret now," he assured his prisoner. "When I get me money, yer free ta go. I don't mean ya no harm." He closed the door firmly behind him, turning the key in the rusty lock.

Mr. Hazelton-Smythe looked around him in dismay. During the past few days that he had been incarcerated here, he had tried various methods to escape. The door, as he had learned his first day, was old but very strong, and the lock was quite secure. There was one little window that looked down over the street, but it was too small for him to fit through, even if it hadn't been too high to jump from. He had tried to catch someone's attention on the street and thereby secure his release, but in this squalid section of town no one cared to inquire about a man waving from a window. He had resigned himself to the fact that his release was going to have to be through the door, and probably with Mr. Heggit's approval.

Mr. Hazelton-Smythe had tried to solve the riddle of who his abductor had been, but he knew of no one that had such a grudge against him. He was also anxious to see Sir Giles to arrange his marriage so he could be sure of inheriting Lady Ffoulkes's fortune. He thought for a moment, wondering if the chasing around and the abduction could in any way be related. He didn't see how, though, for the one fellow had been a friend of Julia's. He couldn't recall his name, but he had been at his aunt's party. Surely she would not entertain abductors in her house. Mr. Hazelton-Smythe shook his head in confusion. It was all too puzzling, and his environment was too disgusting to be able to give his full concentration to the matter. He took out his handkerchief and tried to revive the shine on his boots.

Mrs. Sigsby was delighted to see the girls. She carefully placed Phoebe between herself and her son, while Julia chose a chair on her own.

When they had left Lady Ffoulkes's room, Phoebe had been ready for tears again, but Julia had talked sensibly with her. "We know how much time is left," she had reminded her, "and we'll find a way for you and Muffin to get together, so don't let Cecil worry you."

Phoebe had seemed in better spirits as they had eaten breakfast, and Julia had spent the time making decisions about her own future. She knew that she could not marry the man she loved as he loved another and she did not want anyone else. In Julia's mind that left only one alternative—to get some form of employment. The jobs open to girls of her age and upbringing were not too varied, so it would mean either becoming a governess or a companion to an elderly lady. She had seen an employment agency on Fleet Street and was determined to visit it soon. She would wait until Phoebe and Muffin were settled and then she would begin her new life in service.

"Cecil has a lovely home in Bristol," Mrs. Sigsby brought Julia back to the present time.

"Oh?" said Julia, while Phoebe tried to smile appreciatively.

"He inherited it from his godfather," she added, while Cecil stared at the floor.

"I've never been to Bristol," Phoebe said.

"His godfather left him very well off," Mrs. Sigsby boasted. "He probably did not mention it, but money is no problem to him." She smiled down at the back of his head, which was all they could see of him. "He doesn't like to boast, you know."

Phoebe nodded.

"He's such a popular young man," Mrs. Sigsby went on. "Why the girls are always fussing over him. It's not just the house or the money, you know. He just has a way with women. He has that certain kind of attraction. Some days he is just worn out with all the attention." She reached over and patted his shoulder consolingly. "It can be very hard having all that charm."

Mrs. Sigsby invited the girls to stay for lunch, but they declined politely saying they had to get ready for a party at the Ashtons' that evening. Neither of them was planning on spending all afternoon in preparation, but Mrs. Sigsby did not find their excuse strange, and soon Cecil was escorting them back to Bolton Street.

By eleven o'clock that evening Julia was quite tired of smiling and pretending to enjoy herself. It was all Marc's fault, she told herself crossly. For he seemed to be watching her constantly, and she was forced to smile happily and flirt with whomever she was near to convince him that he needn't feel sorry for her. She wished he would go back to Claudia who was sitting forlornly next to her mother. Julia had seen him dance with her once, but since then he seemed to be unaware of her.

Deciding that Claudia was not her problem, she

reached over and playfully tapped Lt. Lyndon on the wrist. "I thought you were going to get me a glass of champagne," she teased him.

"Oh, yes," he remembered suddenly, and jumped up to get it.

Julia watched him go, wondering if everyone got depressed and forgetful as the season came to a close.

"Alone at last, Miss Henley?" Sir Tristan asked as he sat down next to Julia.

"Not any longer," she laughed.

"You must be the most popular lady here," he complained. "I've been waiting over an hour to speak to you."

"That's quite sad," Julia sighed sympathetically.

"Have you saved me a dance?"

"Now, really," she laughed. "Wouldn't you suppose that as the most popular lady here, I would have filled my card already?"

He nodded sadly. "Perhaps you would be willing to forget one of them for me. I'm sure that no one on that silly list cares for you the way I do."

Julia smiled but shook her head. "That wouldn't be very polite of me."

"At least give me a little of your time, then," he pleaded earnestly. "I didn't speak at Vauxhall because you were so upset, but you can't expect me to wait this evening because you have promised to dance with some others."

Julia felt wretched but she truly did not want to give him the chance to speak to her. If he did so, it would only mean that she would have to hurt him by refusing his offer, and she liked him too well to see him hurt.

"I will take you to dinner," he decided. "After we have eaten, we will steal away and I will be able to open my heart to you."

The light he saw in Julia's eyes was because of happiness, he decided, as he gave her hand a small squeeze where it lay on the settee next to her. "Until later, then," he said as he left, not knowing the only emotion Julia was feeling was one of relief that an unpleasant scene had been avoided for now.

Julia still could see no sign of Lt. Lyndon returning and felt uneasy about sitting alone, so she moved over slightly to be near some other young ladies who were sitting close to her. Although she pretended an interest in their conversation, her mind kept drifting back to Sir Tristan and the likelihood of his making her an offer.

Much as she liked and respected Sir Tristan, she did not love him and knew that she could not marry him. He would be more acceptable than Mr. Hazelton-Smythe, but it still would not be enough. Her feelings for Marc were so strong that she could not contemplate a marriage in which those feelings would have no place. She belonged to Marc in her mind, and she could not give her body to someone else. She would just have to try to let Sir Tristan down gently.

Very soon, Julia felt someone sit down at her side. She was surprised to see it was Lady Ffoulkes, not Lt. Lyndon.

"You had better be careful," Lady Ffoulkes warned her. "I don't know how you came to meet such a one as Sir Tristan, but Lady Ruskin warned me about him."

Julia looked at her questioningly.

"He's run through several fortunes and is a real gambler. He only talks to a woman if she has money, or is his mistress. Everyone knows that you have no money, so if you aren't careful, they'll think that you're fast and loose, and your reputation will be gone."

With that she was up and away before Julia had any time to argue.

Julia sat staring at the couples dancing, but not really seeing anything. She felt like a perfect flat. A green, inexperienced country bumpkin. She never for a moment doubted what Lady Ffoulkes had told her. It made too much sense. Sir Tristan had thought she was an heiress and had played upon her inexperience.

Julia knew now why he never called on her at home and never wanted to be seen with her in public. He was afraid that someone might warn her about him. She even remembered his little speech when they were at the theater, warning her against

147

the gossip she might hear. He had expected that she would believe all that nonsense about her charm and beauty.

The more she thought about his treachery, the angrier she became. It was all a game to him, she thought. He played his charm and flattery against her inexperience. The prize was her fortune. She smiled suddenly. Of course, the joke was on him, for she had no fortune.

Julia remembered their first meeting and how angry she had been with Phoebe for giving a false impression of their wealth, and how sympathetic Sir Tristan had been. How naive she and Phoebe were!

With a shock Julia realized that the line of dancers had parted and she was staring right across the floor at Sir Tristan. She must have been smiling at the thought of her lack of fortune, for he smiled back at her. Her first thought was to turn away coldly, but then she had another idea and smiled even more sweetly at him. Let him think she was besotted with him, she told herself. He deserved to waste his time courting an almost penniless girl, for she was under no obligation to reveal her lack of fortune to him. He had tried to trick her, but she would do nothing so dastardly. She would only be friendly and polite. Let him interpret that as he liked, she thought, laughing to herself.

Were all men so untrustworthy? she wondered as she absently played with her fan. It appeared so. But she had learned her lesson. She would trust none of them. She would find herself a job and be independent. She was not about to let herself be fooled by anyone again.

Lt. Lyndon finally returned, and Julia forced herself to look glad to see him.

"Devil of a time getting through the crowds," he apologized as he handed her the glass of champagne.

Julia sipped the drink slowly, using the time to get her feelings under control, but the taste of the drink made her cough.

"Don't like it, eh?" Lt. Lyndon asked, taking the drink from her hand. "Takes a while to get used to." He tipped the glass and finished what was left.

"My, you must have been thirsty," Julia said as he lowered the glass.

"Fact is, Miss Henley," he confided, "I'm not happy."

Since he had looked miserable all evening, this came as no surprise to Julia.

"Is there anything I can do?" she asked politely, hoping that he would say no and take himself off somewhere else to be miserable.

"Maybe you could," he said hopefully. "Maybe you'd understand these things better."

A young man came up to ask Julia to dance. "Sorry, old man," Lt. Lyndon said. "It's my dance."

The young man went away and the lieutenant turned to Julia. "Could we go someplace where we could talk?"

Julia nodded reluctantly, and they searched for a deserted anteroom.

They were barely settled on a sofa in a quiet little room when the lieutenant began. "I'm in love," he announced mournfully.

Julia was not sure what response was expected, but his melancholy attitude seemed to indicate sympathy. "I'm sorry," she murmured.

"Oh, no," he insisted. "It's wonderful. It has made me very happy."

"But you don't look happy," Julia hesitated to point out.

"That's all my fault," he told her. "I met this wonderful girl. An angel. A beautiful goddess. The loveliest girl in London."

"Yes, I understand," Julia interrupted. "She's very lovely. But why are you unhappy?"

"I must have done something to displease her," Lt. Lyndon said. "I'm not sure what, but I know it has to be my fault. She's too good a person to have just been toying with my affections. She's too honest, you see. Too loyal."

"I really don't understand," Julia interrupted again. "Maybe you should explain a little more."

He nodded morosely. "We met early in the season, and I knew I was in love right away. I don't have a fortune, and I'm not likely to inherit one, but she didn't seem to mind. Some girls do, you know," he added. "But she's not like that. She's too unworldly." Julia sighed impatiently, so he continued. "I was sure that she was beginning to care about me just last week. I saw her quite often, almost every day, and I thought I could detect a fondness in her speech to me. I was delighted. I thought that perhaps in a few months I might be able to approach her father."

"A few months?" Julia said in surprise. "Why were you going to wait a few months?"

"I didn't want to rush her," he explained patiently. "You see, she's—"

Julia did not wish to hear another litany of her praises. "Mightn't she begin to doubt your sincerity if you wait so long to make a declaration?"

"Oh, no," he was positive. "She's so innocent that I must give her time to adjust to me."

Julia thought this paragon sounded rather insufferable, and felt like advising the lieutenant to find someone else.

"In the last few days, though, she has been very cold to me and seems to prefer the company of others." He stood up and walked over to the window. "I don't know what I have done to offend her, but I fear it was that I held her hand as I said good night to her last time she was at Almacks."

"I really doubt that holding her hand would offend her," Julia tried to convince him. "If she's old enough to be having a season, she's surely had her hand held before."

Lt. Lyndon turned around, looking quite shocked. "How can you say such a thing!" he demanded of her. "She's not like most of the women you meet. She's pure and innocent." He turned back to the window. "Oh, if only my regiment were to be sent to France. Perhaps if I died heroically in battle, she would appreciate me more."

Julia had had enough. "This is all quite silly!" she said impatiently. "She probably got tired of your dilly-dallying around and decided you were the one who was only flirting. If you love her so much, you must tell her. Make her listen to you."

"Maybe you're right," he said hesitantly. "Although I was sure that she knew how I felt."

"Have you ever told her?" Julia demanded.

He shook his head. "But she must have known."

"Tell her," Julia repeated. "Convince her that you love her, and only her. That you've always loved her and that you always will."

"You're right," he said, suddenly full of enthusiasm. "I'll get her alone, and I'll make her decide whether she wants to marry me or not." He was very determined. "I'll do it now," he announced, then seemed to remember her presence. "Gosh, Miss Henley, you're a gem," he said, taking her hand. "I can never thank you enough for your advice." He leaned over and gave her a quick kiss on the cheek.

"Julia!"

The two of them turned in the direction of the shriek and saw Lady Ffoulkes clutching the doorway as if she might faint.

"I can explain, Lady Ffoulkes," Lt. Lyndon said quickly.

"No," Julia insisted. "I'll explain. You just go."

He was not sure if he should obey, but Lady Ffoulkes informed him that he was going to stay. "You can't just compromise my ward and leave," she said. "Everyone noticed your absence, Julia, so I came looking for you. But I never thought to find you in here, with this . . . this . . . person."

Lt. Lyndon was looking more and more upset by the moment.

"It was really nothing," Julia tried to explain. "We were merely talking."

"You were not talking when I came in, child," she reminded her.

Julia realized that what she said was true, so she remained silent.

Lady Ffoulkes came further into the room and sank into a chair, as if she did not have the strength to move anymore. She had, however, chosen a chair between the lieutenant and the door.

"It's not that I blame you, Julia," she said sadly, taking a small lace handkerchief from her pocket. "You have no real experience of the life one leads in London." She dabbed daintily at her eyes to wipe away some imaginary tears. "But to end up the prey of some evil-minded man is just too much to bear." She put her handkerchief up to her face again, but was careful that it did not block her vision.

"The lieutenant . . . ," Julia began, but was interrupted by him.

"She is right, Julia," he said to her quietly. Then he turned to Lady Ffoulkes. "Just before you came in," he told her, "Miss Henley had consented to become my wife. I hope you will excuse the fact that I spoke to her before I spoke to Sir Giles, but perhaps you can understand that my heart was too full to wait," he added mournfully.

Julia stared at him in disbelief, wondering if he had taken leave of his senses, but Lady Ffoulkes made a remarkable recovery from her attack of the vapors.

"He should be back in town in a day or two," she told him. "You can talk to him then and get it all set down on paper."

Lt. Lyndon nodded in a manner reminiscent of the martyrs going to their deaths, as Lady Ffoulkes ushered Julia out the door.

"I think we've had enough excitement for one night," she told Julia. "We'll find your sister and go home."

* * *

Lady Ffoulkes did not mention Julia's engagement on the way home, and Julia was quite relieved. Hopefully the lieutenant would call the next day and they could contrive a way to end this ridiculous betrothal. The less people who knew about it the better, Julia felt as they entered the house.

Much to their surprise, waiting in the hall for them to return was Mr. Hazelton-Smythe. At least, Julia thought it was him. He was wearing filthy clothes that reeked of garlic, onions, and things that she could not identify.

Lady Ffoulkes took one look at him, sent a very curious Phoebe up to her room, and ushered her nephew and Julia into the sitting room.

"But don't you dare sit in here," she warned him. "It might be even better if you were to stand by the window," she ordered.

With a loud sigh he did as he was told, which took him far enough away so his smell was not quite so overpowering.

"Where did you get those clothes?" Lady Ffoulkes demanded. "And why do you think you can come calling on me dressed like that?"

Julia feared that the worst offense was coming to the house in them, not actually wearing them.

"I was abducted," Mr. Hazelton-Smythe cried indignantly. "I have been missing for days and I'll wager that no one even inquired about my whereabouts." He looked quite injured when no one rushed over to him with sympathy.

"As I recall, you were missing a good part of last week, too," Lady Ffoulkes reminded him. When he made no comment, she continued. "Who abducted you? And why?"

"I don't know who," he answered, "and I don't know why, but I would assume that you might show a little interest in your only relative's wellbeing. You don't seem to care how I survived my ordeal, just so I don't soil your chairs."

Julia thought he had a point, but Lady Ffoulkes didn't.

"You smell like you survived with the frequent help of gin," she commented dryly, identifying the unknown smell for Julia. "Did they decide that you weren't worth the trouble and let you go?"

"I escaped by my wits," he said proudly. "I convinced my captor to free me by giving him all my clothes, which he had admired. Even my new boots with the gold tassels," he added sadly.

Julia almost burst out laughing, but managed to change it into a cough. Lady Ffoulkes glanced at her as if she had just remembered her presence. "Did all this happen before you saw Sir Giles or after?" she asked.

"Before," he cried angrily. "I almost think it was part of a plot to keep me from seeing him. I shall be much more careful when I go to see him the next time."

"You don't have to," Lady Ffoulkes said with a short laugh. "Julia here got herself engaged tonight, so you're just a bit too late."

"She what!" Harold yelled. "And you let her?" He did not know whom he was angrier at, but turned to his aunt, "That's not fair. We had an understanding. I was going to marry her," he pouted.

But Lady Ffoulkes just shrugged her shoulders. "You took too long," she said.

Harold could not believe that he had lost out. "But Aunt Primrose," he whined.

"Sorry, Harold," she said coldly. "You lose."

Harold was in such shock that he suddenly sat down in one of Lady Ffoulkes's damask chairs.

"Get up, you filthy boy!" Lady Ffoulkes screamed at him. "Now I'll have to get that cleaned at once." She hurried out into the hall calling for a maid, all of whom were no doubt in bed.

Mr. Hazelton-Smythe walked over to where Julia stood. She was not afraid of him, but he smelled so bad that she backed away.

"How could you accept another man's proposal when we were to be married?" he asked, quite the injured party.

"But we weren't," she reminded him. "You never

asked me, but I told you anyway that I would not marry you. I told you several times and I meant it."

"But you can't do this to me," he pleaded. "Aunt Primrose would have been so pleased had I taken one of you off her hands that I would have been sure to inherit all her money. Now who knows what she'll do with it. It's just not fair!" he cried.

Julia wondered why she had never thought of that reason for his determined courting of her.

Lady Ffoulkes reentered the room with a maid tagging along behind. She seemed surprised to see both her nephew and Julia still in the room. "Get along, will you both," she cried, more concerned with the state of her chair.

Mr. Hazelton-Smythe turned to Julia. "When you realize that this betrothal of yours is a mistake, you may contact me at my lodgings in Bury Street." He bowed solemnly and made his way out the door.

His dignified exit was marred somewhat, for the maid got a whiff of him as he passed and said rather loudly, "Cor, he's a ripe one, ain't he?"

CHAPTER NINE

"But no one knows of it yet," Julia pleaded with Lt. Lyndon the next morning. "Now is the time to break off the engagement."

"But why should we break it off?" he asked, quite puzzled.

Julia rose from her chair, so agitated that she could not sit still. She had slept little the night before, but eventually had managed to convince herself that if the lieutenant would just come calling the next day, they would resolve all their problems. Now he had come but was stubbornly refusing to see her side of the problem.

Julia paced the floor of the small sitting room that Lady Ffoulkes had let them use. It was decorated in cheerful yellows and greens, but Lt. Lyndon was not letting it affect his melancholy expression. He sat in a small chair near the door and stared glumly at his hands.

"You surely must see that it wouldn't do at all," Julia repeated. She realized that she had been clutching her skirt nervously, and tried unsuccessfully to smooth out the wrinkled fabric.

"I've been thinking, Miss Henley," he said slowly, not even looking at her. "I think it might be just the thing. I daresay that we could manage to get along tolerably well."

Julia sank back into her chair. "But you're in love with someone else," she pointed out. "You know you don't really want to marry me."

The lieutenant wrung his hands together, then looked over at her. "Fact is, I've thought a lot about that, too. I know that she doesn't love me. It stands to reason that somebody as lovely as her wouldn't care about me. So I'm willing to marry you."

Julia looked at him in stunned silence for a moment. "My that was nicely put," she commented dryly.

Lt. Lyndon blushed as he realized that his last remark was far from complimentary. "I'm sorry," he said sincerely. "I meant no insult. It's just that . . ."

Julia waved aside his apology. "I know, I know. I'm not the person you love and it's hard to accept anyone else."

He nodded morosely.

"That's just why we must call this off," Julia persisted. "Now, before too many people learn of it. Neither one of us deserves to be pushed into a marriage like this. You must give your love a chance. You don't know how she feels about you."

He nodded and Julia felt he was close to agreeing, so she pushed on with her argument. "I thought you were determined to find out what her true feelings about you were, and you have to be free to do that."

Her reminder of their conversation from last night was a mistake, though, for his face clouded over at the memory. "No, it doesn't matter anymore," he said quickly. "I've compromised you and I have to marry you. Your reputation is at stake. I won't allow you to sacrifice it for me." He stood up, his decision made. "As soon as your guardian returns, I'll see him. We'll marry soon."

He sat down next to her, and picking up one of her hands, patted it gently. "You'll see, Miss Henley. It will work out well. I'll do everything I can to make you happy."

His speech might have had a greater effect on Julia had he not looked so forlorn as he said it. Julia had no chance to reply, though, for Lady Ffoulkes chose that moment to enter. The lieutenant dropped Julia's hand guiltily and jumped to his feet.

"Oh, must you go so soon?" Lady Ffoulkes asked, assuming that he was on his feet because of his imminent departure. "We still have so many details to be worked out."

The lieutenant bowed slightly toward her. "I assure you I will see Sir Giles as soon as it is possible, so there will be no delay in the wedding. I was just telling Miss Henley that I would send the announcement to the Gazette this morning."

"Yes, that must be done," Lady Ffoulkes nodded happily. "But you needn't call her Miss Henley now that you're to be married. I'm sure that you aren't that formal when you're alone together," she laughed coyly.

"True," he said. Turning to Julia, he picked up her hand and held it lightly. "Good day, Julia," he said hesitantly. "I expect I'll see you soon." He bent down and kissed her hand.

"Good-bye, John," Julia sighed.

He bowed to Lady Ffoulkes, then left the room.

Lady Ffoulkes watched him leave. "You've done fairly well for yourself," she congratulated Julia. "I just hope we can settle your sister as well."

Julia nodded in half-hearted agreement, for she was quite sure that Lady Ffoulkes was not the one to approach with her resolution not to marry John. She excused herself and went up to her room where she would be able to think in peace.

However, when she entered the room, she found Phoebe sitting in a chair, looking quite glum.

She looked up as her sister entered. "Oh, Julia. Who came to call? Did anyone want to see me?" she asked hopefully.

"No," Julia said as she sat down on the edge of the bed. "It was Lieutenant Lyndon. He came to see me."

Phoebe lost a little of her depression. "He seems to be very attentive lately," she teased.

Last night Julia had resolved to talk Lt. Lyndon out of their ridiculous engagement, but now she feared there was little chance of that. Since Phoebe was bound to learn of it sometime, Julia decided to tell her herself.

"Yes," Julia admitted. "We, uh we became engaged last night," she said quickly, forcing herself to smile.

"Oh, Julia, that's wonderful," Phoebe cried, happily hugging her sister. "You must be very happy."

Julia remembered Phoebe's unhappiness when she had come into the room and knew that she was worried about her own future. It wouldn't be fair for Julia to burden her with her problems, too. "Yes, it's very exciting," Julia said. "But since Sir Giles isn't here, it isn't really official yet."

"There won't be any problem in getting him to agree, will there?" Phoebe asked. "Oh, and now you're free of Harold," she suddenly remembered. "Did you tell him last night? I'll bet he was really upset," she laughed.

"He wasn't too happy," Julia admitted. "But it was because he had hoped to inherit Lady Ffoulkes's wealth if he helped her out by marrying me."

Phoebe stared at her in astonishment for a few minutes. "Why that's terrible!" she cried angrily.

"I'm glad that he lost out to Lieutenant Lyndon. He's so much nicer, anyway. I just hope that I can find someone other than Mr. Sigsby," she added glumly. "I don't think he's doing it for Lady Ffoulkes's money, but I'd really rather not marry him."

"Has Muffin said anything to you that would make you think he might offer for you?" Julia asked.

Phoebe shook her head. "If only there was some way to force him into offering for me. Oh, I know that sounds terrible," she hurried to say. "But I really think he cares for me. He's just too shy to speak."

Julia had a strange expression on her face, and Phoebe feared that she was shocked by what she had said. "I was just thinking out loud," Phoebe said quickly. "I don't want to marry Mr. Sigsby, but I don't actually want to force Muffin to marry me."

"Why not?"

It was Phoebe's turn to look shocked. "That wouldn't be right," she managed to stutter. "I couldn't force him to do something that he didn't want to do. Besides," she added, "I wouldn't know how."

"You said yourself that he cares about you, and I agree. He's very attentive and always speaks very highly of you. I don't think force would be necessary. All you would have to do is push him a bit."

"Push him how?"

Julia did not want to divulge the circumstances of her own engagement, so she tried to sound vague. "All you have to do is make it appear that he has compromised you. Lady Ffoulkes would do the rest."

Phoebe was looking highly skeptical, so Julia explained further. "Get him to take you into an anteroom at the musicale tonight, or at the ball later this week. I'll try to get Lady Ffoulkes there, and she'll assume the worst."

"But he'll never agree to go there with me. He's far too proper. There have been a few men I've danced with who have tried to take me into one of them, but never Muffin." Phoebe giggled suddenly. "I think he'd be quite shocked were I to suggest it."

"It doesn't have to be improper," Julia insisted. "If you felt faint, wouldn't he help you to a place where you could rest?"

Phoebe's eyes sparkled. "I'm sure he would," she laughed. "I know he would." She jumped up and hugged Julia happily, full of confidence. "Oh, I just know this will all work. Thank you so much, Julia. Now, we're both going to be so happy."

That evening the girls and Lady Ffoulkes were going to a musicale at the home of a Lady

Wycherley. She was an old friend of Lady Ffoulkes and also happened to be Lady Annabella Tippet's godmother.

They had met Lady Wycherley one afternoon when they had been driving through Hyde Park with Lady Ffoulkes. Just as they had been leaving the park, a rich-looking barouche had pulled alongside of them. The girls had recognized Lady Wycherley and her companion Lady Annabella who had been much too busy not noticing the men nearby to see Julia and Phoebe.

"I do hope you are coming to my musicale," Lady Wycherley had said. "My darling Annabella, here," she had paused to pat her hand, "is going to treat us to some music on her harp. She's quite accomplished but hesitates to play in public because she's so modest."

"Darling Annabella" blushed prettily and had said, quite insincerely, "I'm not really that good. I usually just play for my own enjoyment." She had paused before turning to the girls. "Perhaps you girls would like to perform at the musicale, also?"

She had smiled in a rather superior way as the girls hastily refused, then she and her godmother had gone on their way.

If it had not been for her hope that she would see Muffin that night, Phoebe would have been reluctant to attend. But she had decided to try Julia's idea that evening and so planned her evening with care.

The dress she chose was a pale cream silk brocade. It had been an unfortunate color choice, for it made her look washed out and pale, but it seemed perfect for her plot. Once she had it on, though, it was obvious that it wasn't enough to make her look ill, for excitement put a definite sparkle in her eyes and gave a healthy glow to her skin.

Phoebe sighed and sat down to think. She could hardly claim to be ill when she looked the picture of health. She had a sudden idea and rummaged through the base of her wardrobe for her drawing case, for amid the paper and paints in it there was also a piece of white chalk. She found the chalk with relative ease and rubbed some of its whiteness onto her fingertips. Then she smoothed it onto her face.

But when she looked into the mirror, she was not satisfied with the results. She looked more like a ghost than someone who was merely feeling faint. A little scrubbing with a towel removed most of the chalk, but left her still looking paler than usual. "That should do it," she whispered to herself.

Phoebe left her room but waited at the top of the stairs until she could hear Lady Ffoulkes complaining to Julia about how late Phoebe was. Then she hurried down, pulling her pelisse close around her. She hoped Lady Ffoulkes would not notice her pallor and send her back to bed.

But Lady Ffoulkes was too busy hurrying them out the door to take any notice of Phoebe. The carriage was dark, and when they entered Lady Wycherley's home, Lady Ffoulkes was kept busy greeting her friends, so Julia and Phoebe were able to slip off to find some of the younger people. The first person they met was Marc.

"Hello, girls," he said brightly, coming over to join them. He stopped and took a closer look at Phoebe. "What's the matter with you?" he asked ungallantly. "You look like you're half dead."

"That's hardly the thing to tell a girl," Phoebe pouted. "I'm just a trifle tired, that's all." Might as well start the act immediately, she thought.

Marc looked unconvinced. "You shouldn't have come if you were sick," he scolded her unsympathetically. "It's lucky that Muffin won't see you looking like that or he'd never come to call on you."

"What do you mean he won't see it? Isn't he here?" Phoebe looked worried.

"No," Marc shook his head. "Hates these affairs." He leaned forward so only the girls could hear him. "Especially harp music."

"That's awful," Phoebe muttered under her breath.

"Why?" Marc was puzzled. "You don't play the harp, do you?"

"I'm sure that you'll see him soon," Julia tried to offer a word of comfort. "She enjoys his company and hoped to see him tonight," Julia explained to Marc.

Marc, however, was busy watching Phoebe as she angrily tapped her pale blue fan against her cheek, trying rapidly to revise her plans. "I hate to be the one to mention this," Marc said quietly, "but your illness seems to be coming off on your fan."

Phoebe looked down at it in horror and up at Marc's eyes brimming with laughter.

"Maybe you should rest for a few minutes," Julia suggested, nodding toward the stairs.

Phoebe understood her, and excusing herself, quickly dashed up the stairs to wash her face.

"You're looking quite lovely tonight," Marc said to Julia as they stood by themselves for a few minutes.

"Thank you," Julia smiled slightly. She had not really talked to Marc since that night at Vauxhall when she had told him that she loved someone else. Now she was not sure what to say to him, but was certain that she would not mention her engagement.

A crowd of people entering the drawing room saved her from making any response, for they were suddenly surrounded by friends. Julia was busy greeting them, but her mind was not on it. She was more concerned with her own problems.

Julia had already decided that once Phoebe was safely engaged to Muffin she would break off her engagement to Lt. Lyndon. If all went well, she would have a job waiting for her. The thought of leaving Phoebe and having to work for her living, having her time owned by someone else, was not too pleasing, but she tried not to think of that part of it. At least she would not be tied down to someone she did not love.

Julia tried to console herself with the thought that if she was working she would no longer move in the same circles as Marc and would not be forced to see him and Claudia together as husband and wife. But the thought of not seeing Marc again failed to cheer her up.

"The season's almost over," Marc said brightly.

Julia looked up in surprise. She had not been aware that they were alone again. "Yes, it is," she said, noticing his cheerfulness. Did it mean that he and Claudia had reconciled?

"There's always such a mad rush at the end of the season," he laughed. "You'd think it was because no one was going to see anybody else for months, but the same people will be in Brighton together, and in Bath." Why was he so cheerful? Julia wondered.

Marc's good spirits were due solely to the fact that he remembered that Lady Ffoulkes wanted Julia married by the end of the season. So far he had not noticed anyone being especially attentive to her, even though she had said she had fallen in love. If she had been so unfortunate as to have formed an attachment for someone unsuitable, then Marc was quite ready to step in. He would approach Sir Giles soon and ask for her hand. Marc was quite aware of the fact that she did not love him, but if she had to be married, and couldn't have the one she loved, then at least she could have someone who loved her.

Lady Wycherley had hired a musician to play some pieces before Annabella was to play, and he was taking his place at the piano when Phoebe returned. Trailing a little behind her was Lt. Lyndon.

"You've made a remarkable recovery," Marc teased when he saw her normal blushing cheeks.

Phoebe gave him a dark look and turned to Julia. "Look who found me wandering about," she said as Lt. Lyndon joined them.

Julia smiled weakly at him as Marc greeted him happily. Marc did not notice that he was alone in his enthusiasm.

The pianist began to warm up and Lady Wycherley tried to shoo everyone into the salon so they could begin. Marc led the way, trying to find a place where the four of them could sit together, but there were no empty places large enough.

"We'll have to split up," he said to Phoebe who was right behind him. He did not mind, for that would give him more of a chance to be with Julia without close friends nearby to distract her.

Marc spotted two places on a small settee near the wall in a rather secluded spot and made his way toward them. He turned to point them out to Julia, only to discover that Phoebe was the only one there. He looked around him in puzzlement.

"They're sitting back there," Phoebe said, and nodded to some seats Marc had already passed. There were Lt. Lyndon and Julia sitting and talking together as if they were alone in the world.

"Oh," was all Marc said, conscious of a sinking feeling in the pit of his stomach. He suddenly remembered that Phoebe was still there and started to lead her to the seats, but someone else had already taken them.

In the end he and Phoebe had to sit in the very front because those were the only places left.

The pianist was quite talented and it was pleasant to listen to him, but by the end of his fourth piece Julia was ready for him to finish. John was sitting dutifully at her side, making things even more intolerable. He must have read somewhere that a fiancé is solicitous of his intended, for he was constantly asking about her comfort.

No, she was not too warm. No, she was not too cool. Yes, she was quite comfortable where she was sitting. No, she did not want to exchange places with him. Yes, she was enjoying the music. The only place she would rather be was far from him, she thought crossly.

Besides questioning her comfort, Lt. Lyndon spent his time searching the crowd. Julia did not bother to ask whom he was looking for. She knew quite well that he was hoping to see that nameless woman he loved. Julia only wished she knew which girl it was because if she did, she might find a way to end her own ridiculous engagement. Apparently, though, his search was not successful, for he continued to look as mournful as ever.

The pianist finally finished his last piece and Lady Wycherley fluttered up to the piano to tell them of the next treat they had in store for them. As she spoke, in a voice that barely carried to the first row of seats, Lady Annabella floated up to her instrument, escorted by three of her favored gallants.

Julia wondered in amusement if she needed all that help to go in front of everyone, but each of the gentlemen had a task to perform. One helped her methodically position her chair, another held her fan, while the third was allowed to hold a small nosegay of white roses that she carried.

Eventually all was arranged to her satisfaction and she began to play. Julia had to admit that she made a pleasing picture in her flowing white dress, and she expected that the enthusiastic response was more in appreciation of that than her playing. Julia merely appreciated the fact that she did not play very long.

"Why don't we get some refreshments?" John suggested as the music ended.

Julia took his arm and he led her into the dining room. A long table ran the length of the room, piled high with a wide variety of food. There were lobster patties, shrimp cakes, six different kinds of small sandwiches, and a tempting array of sweets. They quickly filled their plates and found an empty table on the terrace. As they sat down a footman hurried over to pour glasses of punch for them.

"I fear harp music isn't a favorite of mine," the lieutenant apologized.

Julia shook her head and smiled. "It was very popular among the girls I went to school with."

Neither of them seemed to know what to say next, so they began to eat quickly. Suddenly, Julia was aware of someone standing near them. She looked up to see Marc and Claudia standing next to the table.

"May we join you?" Marc asked.

"Of course," John mumbled, and moved his chair closer to Julia to make room for them.

"Good music, wasn't it?" Marc asked as he sat down. The evening was not proceeding as he had planned. First Julia had been stranded with Lyndon, then Claudia had attached herself to him. Still, he hoped that he might get some time with Julia yet.

"I do like harp music," Claudia said anxiously.

"Oh, yes. It was beautiful," John agreed, much to Julia's astonishment. She tried not to stare at him as the conversation dwindled down to an awkward silence.

As Julia drank the last of her punch she heard a voice next to her. "Good evening, Miss Henley." She looked up in surprise to see Mr. Hazelton-Smythe standing next to the table.

"Oh, hello," she said politely. "I didn't see you here earlier."

"I am flattered to think that you were looking for me," he bowed slightly, then looked a trifle ill at ease. "Actually I wanted to apologize to you for my behavior last night." He looked around him at the others at the table, hoping they might leave and let him proceed in privacy, but they were settled where they were, quite curious to hear what he would say next.

He coughed uncomfortably and turned back to Julia, trying to ignore the others. "I fear I may have been a bit rude, but, you see, I was so shocked by the news of your engagement that my feelings overcame my good sense."

"Your engagement!" Marc interrupted, half rising from his chair and turning to Julia. "When did you become engaged?"

John put his arm protectively around Julia's shoulders. "Miss Henley and I became engaged last evening," he said defensively.

"You and Julia are going to be married?" Claudia whispered, suddenly quite white.

"Julia!" Marc cried faintly, and sank back into his chair.

Mr. Hazelton-Smythe looked put out that his conversation had been interrupted, and coughed in an attempt to regain Julia's attention. "I left Lady Ffoulkes's home last night before I had the chance to congratulate you and wish you well."

"Thank you," Julia said determinedly. She didn't know why everyone was treating it like a tragedy. John had become uneasy and Marc was looking particularly morose.

Mr. Hazelton-Smythe was not quite finished. "I would like to remind you, though, of my continuing devotion, and hope that if your engagement doesn't work out as you hope that you will let me know." Then he turned and left.

Julia was horribly embarrassed. Although she knew that the feelings he spoke of were disappointment at losing his aunt's fortune, she wished he would not have chosen to speak in front of the others. There was a moment of silence when he left, and Julia stared down at her plate, wishing someone else would speak.

"Oh, look," Claudia cried unexpectedly, and stood up. Julia looked at her in surprise. This was not the type of remark she expected to hear. "There's Mrs. Sefton," Claudia continued cheerfully. "I did so want to speak to her tonight. I hope you will excuse me." She pulled away from the table, looking at Marc hopefully.

Julia stared at her as Marc stood up to join her. "I do hope you'll both be happy," he said quickly. He looked at Julia and she almost expected him to say something else, but he just nodded and led Claudia away.

"We seem to have been deserted rather suddenly," John commented. "Shall we drink to our future?" he asked with a sudden show of cheerfulness, holding up his glass of punch.

"I'm afraid I haven't any left." Julia held up her empty cup.

He just shrugged his shoulders. "Perhaps some other time then," he said.

She nodded as she watched Claudia take Marc's arm and walk very close to him as they left the terrace.

CHAPTER TEN

Julia climbed the stairs in the dark hallway, tightly clutching her small, black reticule. At the top of the stairs was the equally drab, though better lit, office of Miss Worth's Agency for Genteel Employment. Julia pushed open the doorway and timidly entered the office. Outside of a middle-aged woman at a desk, she was the only person there.

The woman at the desk took no notice of her, so Julia sat down on the edge of a wooden chair pushed up against a wall. Julia smoothed down her dress and nervously waited to be spoken to. She was not sure what to expect, since she had never been to an employment agency before, but she hoped her inexperience wasn't noticeable.

Julia had chosen her attire with care, for she knew that her new dresses were much too frivolous and would not impress anyone with her reliability as an employee. Instead, she wore an old black bombazine that she had had made when her grandfather died. Over her severely dressed hair she wore an old poke bonnet trimmed in black ribbons.

Julia looked over at the other woman again, twisting her hands nervously. She had managed to slip out of the house unnoticed, but she knew she would have to return soon or she would surely be missed.

After Julia coughed quietly, the woman at the desk looked up from the paper she was reading. She glanced at Julia, then returned to her paper. A few minutes later, after sighing loudly, the woman struggled to her feet and walked slowly into another room. Then she came back to the doorway and waved Julia forward.

"Miss Worth'll see ya now," she said, and sat down heavily in her chair again.

Julia hurried into Miss Worth's office. She had expected to see a repetition of the outer office but was wrong. Miss Worth's room was painted a soft green and had one comfortable chair placed before a rather imposing desk which seemed to fill the room. At the desk an elderly lady sat. Her body seemed to be cased in wrinkles, but her eyes were flashing and alert. She beckoned Julia forward and motioned for her to sit in the chair.

Julia sat down uncertainly as the woman's eyes took in every detail of her appearance.

"You are looking for a job?" she asked quietly.

Julia nodded.

The woman folded her hands carefully in front of her on the desk. "What kind of employment did you hope to find?"

Julia cleared her throat. "I thought maybe as a governess, or a companion," Julia explained, becoming more nervous.

Miss Worth shook her head silently. "And what qualifications do you have for these jobs?" she asked.

"I speak French," Julia hesitated. "And I could teach needlework." She stopped short as she could think of no more qualifications that she had.

"What is your name?"

"Julia Henley."

"How old are you, Miss Henley?"

"Twenty," Julia lied. Miss Worth's eyebrows rose, but she did not voice her doubts.

"Why is it you wish to find employment?"

Julia looked down at her hands. "I have to," she said simply. "There is no alternative."

"There are always alternatives," Miss Worth chided her gently. "You are too young to go out as a governess. I know that most governesses who are older now once were as young as yourself, but they had an older appearance. You are far too attractive for most women to want you in their households, and I would not place you in the home of a widower."

"What about as a companion?" Julia asked, but without much hope.

"I have no openings," she said. "There are not many positions as a companion open at any time, since most elderly women prefer to have an indigent relative come to stay, rather than hire a stranger."

Julia nodded and began to rise, but Miss Worth waved her back into her seat. "I meant what I said about alternatives," she told Julia.

"You mean as an abigail or a housemaid?" Julia asked.

Miss Worth shook her head. "A young thing like you should get married."

"Oh, no," Julia said, but Miss Worth interrupted.

"There are advertisements in here in every issue," she said, tapping the newspaper on her desk. "Widowers with children looking for a young, healthy wife. They require far less in the way of qualifications than people expect from a governess. Find someone wealthy and you will have an easy life."

"No, that's not what I wanted," Julia said, rising this time. "I want a job, not marriage."

Miss Worth shook her head. "I'm afraid I just can't help you. And be careful of those who say they will," she warned. "I run a respectable establishment, but not everyone does. You might be promised one thing and find yourself in a situation far different."

Julia stood at the door. "Thank you for your

time," she said dejectedly, and left. The woman in the outer room did not even look up as Julia passed through and went back down the stairs.

Julia walked home quickly and managed to slip back into the house without being seen. Apparently Phoebe was still lying down in her room trying to rest after a sleepless night, for Julia did not hear her voice as she ran up the back stairs and into her room.

Quickly changing her clothes, Julia hid them in the bottom of her wardrobe. She unpinned her hair and shook it free. After brushing it briskly, she arranged it in her normal style, all the while telling herself not to become discouraged. She was just as determined not to enter a loveless marriage with John, but she had been counting on getting a job and that looked to be more of a problem than she had thought. She would still look for one, but she was no longer so sure that she would find something.

She rose with a sigh, as she heard voices downstairs. It sounded as if John had come to call, and she would have to make an appearance.

"It had better succeed tonight," Phoebe whispered tersely to Julia as they sat together in the ballroom of the Duke of Haldmere. He was giving a ball for his granddaughter, a rather colorless girl Phoebe and Julia had met only once. The girls were not concerned with the duke or his granddaughter, however, for Phoebe was once again going to try to trap Muffin into offering for her. "He is here tonight," she told Julia. "I saw him come in. Do you remember your part?"

Julia nodded. "I'm to get Lady Ffoulkes when I see you and Muffin leaving the room, and bring her to find you."

"It can't fail tonight because I don't have much time left. We're going to the Sigsbys for dinner tomorrow."

The girls were separated as different men came to claim them for their dances. Julia tried hard to keep an eye on Phoebe, but so far she had not danced with Muffin. She smiled to herself as she thought that perhaps Muffin had some inkling of the plot being laid for him, for he was proving to be very elusive.

Julia was standing up with John for a country dance when she saw Phoebe enter the set with Muffin. Phoebe looked her way and smiled.

Julia managed to watch Phoebe and still perform her steps in the dance. As they were leaving the floor Phoebe appeared to be leaning a bit more heavily on Muffin's arm, and Julia saw them bypass the settee where they had been sitting.

Taking this as her cue, she told John she had to find Lady Ffoulkes. He may have thought her urgency strange, but was too much of a gentleman to question it. He took her arm and led her through the crowd to where Lady Ffoulkes was sitting.

"Lady Ffoulkes," Julia said quietly. "I think Phoebe is ill."

Lady Ffoulkes looked up. Julia was not sure if it was concern or annoyance that caused her expression, but she did not let the thought of either stop her.

"She went into one of the side rooms," Julia continued.

Lady Ffoulkes rose and followed Julia out of the ballroom, with a bewildered John trailing behind.

"I told her not to come if she wasn't well," Lady Ffoulkes muttered to Julia as they looked for Phoebe. They entered one room and embarrassed a couple in a passionate embrace. But it was not Phoebe or Muffin.

"I thought she was feeling better," Julia said as they hurried down the hall.

They went into another room. In it they could see a velvet love seat facing them and the back of a large stuffed chair. There was a branch of candles burning on a table next to the love seat, but the room seemed very dark. Phoebe was sitting on the small sofa, while Muffin stood nearby.

"Phoebe!" Lady Ffoulkes cried. "What is the meaning of this?"

Phoebe looked up but before she could answer a third person rose from the large chair and turned to face them.

"It's quite all right, Primrose," the Dowager Duchess of Ardsley assured her. "Poor Phoebe here was feeling a bit faint and Sir Archibald had the presence of mind to ask me to come to sit with her." She smiled at the newcomers, while Julia could see Phoebe looking disgusted.

"You know, Primrose," the dowager duchess continued. "If her strength does not return, you really should take her to Bath to drink the waters."

Lady Ffoulkes grunted something indistinguishable and turned to Phoebe. "If you aren't well, we had best leave."

Phoebe nodded reluctantly and stood up. Muffin rushed over to her side. "Are you strong enough to get to your carriage alone?" he asked.

"I feel much better," she told him, and turned to the dowager duchess. "Thank you for helping me."

"I was hoping you would go riding with me tomorrow," Muffin said, "but I had better give you a chance to rest."

"I told you that I'm fine now," Phoebe said tersely. She noticed the others looking at her strangely. "Come if you like," she said, trying to sound more pleasant. "I'm sure that I'll feel up to riding with you."

"No, I'll wait, just to be sure you're well." Muffin turned to Lady Ffoulkes. "I'll go ahead and have your carriage brought to the door," he offered. Lady Ffoulkes nodded, so he and Lt. Lyndon left.

Lady Ffoulkes thanked the dowager duchess

politely and walked to the door of the room with her, enduring silently another lecture on the beneficial waters of Bath.

"I should have known it would never work with Muffin," Phoebe whispered to Julia. "Not only did I ruin this evening, but I've spoiled tomorrow, too."

Lady Ffoulkes returned to the girls. "You go ahead and get our cloaks," she told Julia. "Phoebe can rest here for a few more minutes, then we'll meet you at the door."

Julia hurried away. She easily found a maid to get their wraps for them, and she waited in the doorway of a small parlor just off the main entrance hall. She was busily admiring the room's furnishings when she heard a voice behind her.

Julia turned and saw Sir Tristan. With all the fuss over her engagement, she had forgotten about him.

"Julia," he whispered, grabbing her hand and pulling her further into the parlor. "I must talk to you."

By this time the maid had disappeared up the stairs and they were alone. "What do you want?" Julia asked, not bothering to pretend to be pleased to see him.

"How could you do this to me?" he pleaded with her. He clung even more tightly to her hand and refused to let her pull it away. "You knew that I was just waiting to speak to you."

Julia did not pretend to misunderstand him. "I happen to be very fond of John. He's a very nice person."

"So is the prince regent, but that doesn't mean that you have to marry him. After all I've done for you, I would have thought you would have the decency to at least give me a chance."

Julia could not believe his conceit. "Just what have you done for me?" she asked.

"Who do you think managed to rid you of Mr. Hazelton-Smythe's attentions? I went to all that trouble trying to ease things for you, and you snuck around with someone else."

"You had him kidnapped?" Julia asked in a shocked whisper.

Sir Tristan shrugged. "I assume he came to no harm. And I did it for you," he reminded her. "The least you could have done was show a little appreciation."

Julia was stunned. If he was going to such extremes, he must believe she had a tremendous fortune.

"We could be so happy together," he said quietly. "I know you can't possibly care for that Lyndon fellow. Why did you ever accept him?"

"He asked first," she mumbled, still in a daze.

"You mean that your guardian just accepted whoever offered first?" he asked in an angry whisper. "How can you stand for such treatment?

You should be given to the most worthy applicant."

Julia smiled slightly. He made her sound like a rare vase being offered at an auction. "It wasn't just because John was first," she tried to explain. But he let her get no further.

"This is ridiculous," he stated. "You should be allowed to make your own choice. But you mustn't worry, darling, we'll find a way to be rid of your lieutenant."

"You wouldn't harm him?" Julia asked, ignoring the rest of his speech.

"No, I can see that that would distress you."

Julia heard a small cough in the doorway and turned to see that the maid had returned with the cloaks. Past her she could see Lady Ffoulkes talking to someone just inside the ballroom and tried again to pull her hand away. "I must go," she whispered urgently.

But he held her hand too tightly.

"Don't worry, my love, I'll find a way for us to be together." He bent quickly and kissed the inside of her wrist, then let her go. "I will see you soon," he whispered after her.

CHAPTER ELEVEN

"This is the closet where we keep the guest linen," Mrs. Sigsby told Phoebe confidentially.

Phoebe smiled and tried to look interested, but it was becoming more and more difficult. She was being treated to a tour of the Sigsby home, from the attics to the cellars, and the thoroughness of it was rather frightening. Mrs. Sigsby was not treating her like a guest, but more like a daughter, and Phoebe did not like it.

After a rather bland dinner Mrs. Sigsby sat with Lady Ffoulkes in the drawing room, happily making plans for the "big day," while Cecil obediently sat next to Phoebe. Phoebe was clinging tightly to Julia's hand, determined not to be left alone with Cecil for a second.

"Mother was sorry that Sir Giles could not make it here tonight," Cecil said after a long silence.

"He had other plans," Phoebe explained. Actually he had said that getting the girls married was

Primrose's job, not his, so he found something else to do.

"Mother had especially wanted me to see him," Cecil went on.

Phoebe squeezed Julia's hand even tighter and said nothing. She hoped that Lady Ffoulkes would be ready to leave soon, but she was engrossed in conversation and it did not seem likely.

Phoebe, Julia, and Cecil sat in silence a bit longer. Cecil looked extremely ill at ease and kept squirming uncomfortably in his chair. He alternated between wiping his brow with his linen handkerchief and wringing his hands together. He finally decided that his duties as a host demanded that he make one more attempt at conversation.

"Mother says I'm to call on you tomorrow," he said glumly. "She hopes Sir Giles will be home then."

"Oh," Phoebe moaned quietly, while Julia leaned forward.

"He's hardly ever home during the day," she told Cecil confidentially. He looked rather relieved.

"I'll have to call anyway, though," he said after a moment.

Phoebe by this time was trembling with fear and gave up all attempts at conversation. Julia tried a few different topics, but Cecil was not too receptive either.

"Perhaps we could play a game of cards," Julia suggested in desperation. At least it would give them an excuse not to talk.

Cecil jumped at the chance and ran to find some playing cards. A footman came in to prepare the table, while another brought in glasses of lemonade for the girls and poured a glass of wine for Cecil.

When he returned with the cards, the girls suggested several games. They had learned to play a wide number of them from friends at school who had had older brothers to teach them, so Julia and Phoebe were ready to play loo, whist, or even euchre. Unfortunately, Cecil did not know those games, so they had to be content with a rousing game of speculation. It helped to pass the time.

"I've got to do it today," Phoebe whispered to Julia the next morning. John and Muffin had come to call and were taking the girls out riding. "If I don't manage to get an offer from him today, I'll have to marry Cecil, and I won't."

Julia approved of her attitude, but there was no time for Phoebe to explain to her just how she hoped to get an offer from Muffin. As she pulled her horse ahead to ride near him Phoebe looked back at Julia. "Just keep John occupied," she said.

Julia nodded and moved her horse closer to John's. There was a lot that she wanted to say to him. The day was so beautiful she hated to spoil it by the argument that she knew was inevitable, but she could not afford to lose this chance to speak to him in private.

"I really think we ought to call this whole thing off," Julia repeated to him for about the hundredth time. "It's not too late, you know. You could go back to the girl you love."

But John just shook his head, as he always did when she brought the subject up. "Pray, don't mention it," he asked of her. "We will deal very well together, you'll see. Forget that I ever mentioned someone else to you. I have already forgotten her," he added.

Julia sighed. She could not understand his determination to marry her. But she was equally determined not to marry him. It was not proving easy, but she still would find a job, and be independent. She closed her eyes and shook off her worries. It was a sunny, warm day and riding through Green Park, she could almost imagine she was back home in the country.

"What's wrong with your sister's horse?" John asked, breaking into her thoughts.

Julia looked ahead at Phoebe. Her mare did seem to be acting skittish, which was unusual, for it was the mildest of mounts. "I don't know," Julia admitted, surprised that Phoebe had not made any comment about it. Unless, of course, it was all part of her mysterious plan. Julia shook her head in puzzlement.

As they rode through the park Julia kept a close eye on Phoebe and her horse. After its initial skittishness it had quieted down to its normal docile self, stopping occasionally to chew on passing bushes. There seemed to be little danger from that quarter anyway, so Julia turned to John.

"Do we dare let our horses run?" she asked him, longing to feel really free. There was no one there to observe the lapse if they did, for the park was very quiet.

John looked disapproving, so before he had time to answer, Julia gave her horse its head and dashed away under the trees. She could sense that John was close behind her, but she would not let him get too near. This might be one of her last rides for a long time, and she meant to enjoy it. She headed her horse through a narrow opening in the trees to force John to stay behind her.

Once through the trees, she came upon a sudden incline and stopped at the top of it. Stretched out below her was a magnificent view of Buckingham Palace.

"Isn't it beautiful?" Julia sighed as John pulled his horse to a stop near her. "It looks like something out of a fairy tale."

John looked at the panorama spread out before him but was not similarly impressed. "It's nice enough," he shrugged. "But you nearly scared the heart out of me. I didn't know what had happened to you."

"I said I wanted to run," she told him, not in the least affected by his complaints.

"I heard you," he said, grabbing her reins and tugging her horse back, "but I never dreamed you'd actually do it. One does not gallop in town."

"Oh, John," she laughed. "Don't be so stuffy. You have to admit that it gave you a glorious feeling, didn't it?" He nodded grudgingly. "And if anyone asks, you can always say my horse ran away with me."

John shook his head. "You have an answer for everything, don't you?"

The two of them were laughing as they rode back through the trees to find that Phoebe and Muffin were no longer alone. Marc and Claudia had joined them.

"Hello!" Julia called, and urged her horse forward to greet them. John kept pace with her and seemed to be waiting for her to put on a burst of speed again. She caught his eye and laughed.

Marc did not know the cause for Julia's laughter, but assumed it was some private joke that was shared only by Julia and John, so that by the time they reached him, he was glaring at them both.

"Isn't it a glorious day?" Julia asked Marc and Claudia. It was almost like the days she had spent at King's Rest when she and Marc were friends. "It is so wonderful riding here that it makes one—" She stopped suddenly as she realized that she had been about to say it makes one forget all life's problems. She was not going to impose her troubles on anyone else.

"It almost makes one what?" Marc asked, looking at her anxiously. He had been avoiding her since he learned of her engagement, but he could not keep from hoping that she might decide it was a mistake and marry him instead.

"Why, it makes one happy," Julia finished quickly. "What else could it do?" She smiled at everyone in general, hoping that her answer sounded natural, but in Marc's eyes her smile was for John alone.

Why am I fooling myself? Marc thought angrily. Not only did she tell me she was in love with someone else, she's actually engaged to him. How can I still be hoping that she'll come to love me?

"We mustn't stay," Claudia said suddenly. "I have a fitting for a dress very soon, and I have to get back."

Marc looked at her in surprise, for when she had asked him to take her out riding there had been no mention of this appointment. A gentleman, though, could not contradict a lady. "True, we had best be going," he agreed, and nodded to the men. "Phoebe, Julia, I'm sure we'll see you soon." Then he and Claudia were riding back across the park.

The magic of the ride seemed to have gone for Julia. John must have caught her mood, too, for he didn't seem to have much interest in scolding her any further.

"Perhaps we had better turn back, too," he suggested. Julia nodded. Only Phoebe seemed reluctant to leave.

"I wanted to ride a bit more," she said as her horse stopped to munch on yet another bush.

John started to laugh. "I think your horse is more concerned about eating than riding," he said.

Phoebe ignored him and angrily pulled at the reins. Her horse moved reluctantly and continued with the others. Its progress was very slow, though, for it wanted to taste everything along the way.

By the time the girls reached home, Phoebe was barely speaking to anyone. Julia recognized the tight lips and the way she was holding her head as signs that she was close to tears. Julia hurried the others away before Phoebe could actually break down.

"Whatever is wrong, Phoebe?" she asked, rushing her into the drawing room. As soon as the others were out of sight Phoebe began to cry. Julia got her into the drawing room and sat her on the sofa. She pulled out a large handkerchief and gave it to her sister.

"It didn't work," Phoebe sobbed into the square of muslin. "It was my only chance and it didn't work."

"What didn't?" Julia pleaded, aware that Lady Ffoulkes was likely to enter the room at any minute and Phoebe had to get herself under control.

"I put a burr under my horse's saddle," Phoebe admitted between sobs. "He was supposed to bolt with me, and Muffin would save me."

Julia remembered the horse's early skittishness. "It did seem restless at first," she recalled. "But then it seemed to calm down."

"I think the burr fell out," Phoebe wailed.

Julia did not know what to say. She could understand Phoebe's feelings of helplessness, but the way her attempts were misfiring was awfully funny. Trying hard not to give in to the urge to laugh, Julia tried to console her. "You still have time. No one has actually come to offer for you, yet."

Phoebe began to wipe her eyes and smiled slightly at Julia's statement. Maybe there was a bit of hope.

As if on cue the door opened and Lady Ffoulkes appeared. "I thought I heard you girls in here," she said brightly. Too brightly for Julia's peace of mind. Her cheerful look dimmed a bit when she saw Phoebe's red-rimmed eyes. "What's the matter with you?" she asked.

"I got something in my eye," Phoebe said quickly.

"Oh," Lady Ffoulkes said, dismissing it from her mind. "You have a guest," she told Phoebe coyly, and waved for Julia to get up. Phoebe saw Cecil standing behind Lady Ffoulkes, and grabbed Julia's hand tightly.

"Come, come," Lady Ffoulkes said to Cecil. "You mustn't be shy." She pulled him forward and practically pushed him into the room. "Julia, don't you think you ought to change out of your riding habit?"

Julia could not refuse to move, but with Phoebe hanging on to her so tightly, it was hard to do it gracefully. She stood up, but not fast enough for Lady Ffoulkes who grasped her other hand and dragged her toward the door. Phoebe had to let go. "We'll see you both later," Lady Ffoulkes said happily as she closed the door behind her.

Cecil stared at the closed door for a moment, then stared down at Phoebe who was sitting with her head bent. He could only see the top of her head. He cleared his throat, but she did not look up. He coughed again, but still there was no response, so he sat down gingerly at her side.

Cecil had received detailed instructions from his mother on how to propose, and the first step was to hold the lady's hand. It looked like that might be a bit of a problem, for she seemed to be using both of them to clutch at a rather rumpled handkerchief. He sat for a moment wondering if he could skip holding the hand, or if he should wait until one of them was free. He looked at her again and decided it might be some time before she let one dangle loosely at her side. And there was always the chance it would be the one on the other side of her, so he would have to change his position. No, he decided he had better skip that part.

"Miss Phoebe," he said suddenly, his voice breaking in the middle. He cleared his throat and began again. "Miss Phoebe, I have long admired you." He stopped because he thought she had said something. He bent down so he could look into her face.

"Oh, no," she moaned to his surprise, and put the already drenched handkerchief up to her eyes. "Oh, no," she kept repeating.

Cecil was at a loss. This was not one of the reactions his mother had led him to believe girls sometimes had to proposals. He cleared his throat again and decided to modify his approach somewhat. "Miss Phoebe," he began again, "my mother has long admired you."

This got more of a response, for now Phoebe was sobbing openly.

He waited a few minutes, hoping that she would get herself under control, and feeling all the while very uncomfortable. He should have known his mother would make things sound much easier than they were. When Phoebe's sobs had subsided somewhat, he began again.

"I'm sure you know why I'm here," he said, and paused, guessing rightly that there would be more tears. "I do get the feeling that you aren't quite as anxious to marry me as my mother thinks you ought to be," he said after a minute.

Phoebe was still crying but was able to shake her head. "No," she moaned. "I don't really want to."

"Have you told anybody that?"

"Nobody listens," Phoebe sniffed.

Cecil nodded. He had similar problems. "You know," he said confidentially. "I don't really want to marry you, either."

He feared that this might cause another cloudburst, but Phoebe just smiled rather wetly. "You don't?" she asked in disbelief. "That's wonderful."

Cecil shrugged. "I don't see why. My mother still expects me to marry you. If I don't arrange things with Sir Giles, she will."

Phoebe stared at him in astonishment. "Can't you just tell her you won't?" she asked.

He shook his head. "It wouldn't work. Not with my mother."

Phoebe stared at him for a moment, then burst into tears again. "This is even worse," she cried.

Cecil gave her no argument, for he had a strong desire to join her in her tears. Instead he put his head down in his hands and stared moodily at the floor.

Suddenly the door burst open. There was a moment of stunned silence, then Muffin rushed in and grabbed Cecil by his cravat, and pulled him out of his chair.

"What have you done to her, you cad?" he yelled at Cecil's quaking form.

Phoebe had looked up at his entrance and was so delighted by his appearance that she threw herself into his arms, only to continue crying.

The choice of whether to comfort Phoebe or floor Cecil was not hard to make. He let go of Cecil abruptly, allowing him to fall to the floor, for his unsuspecting legs did not seem able to support him. Muffin put his arms around Phoebe and softly patted her back, trying to make her stop crying.

"It's all right, darling," he murmured softly into her hair. "Whatever he's done, I'll make him pay. Just tell me what happened."

For a while all Phoebe could do was cry. Cecil managed to pick himself up and tried to straighten his cravat. "If you'd just let me explain," he began, but was silenced by a fierce stare from Muffin. He decided to remain silent.

Finally Phoebe managed to slow down the flow

long enough to speak. "He wants to marry me," she told Muffin.

"Well to be honest, I don't," Cecil reminded her.

Muffin gathered Phoebe even closer to him, if that was possible, and looked with hatred at poor Cecil. "Oh, you don't?" Muffin snarled at him. "And just what do you want to do, then?"

Much to everyone's surprise, Phoebe began to laugh. Muffin forgot his anger and looked down at his love, fearing that she had become hysterical. It appeared to be quite normal laughter.

"It wasn't like that," she gasped. "He didn't want to make me his mistress. He didn't want anything at all to do with me. It was his mother and my guardian who wanted us to marry."

"Oh," Muffin said as he began to understand.

"Well, my dear Phoebe," Lady Ffoulkes said from the doorway. "How are you and—" She stopped suddenly, as she noticed another person in the room. Someone who had his arms around Cecil's fiancée.

"Just what is going on here?" she demanded. "Do I know you?" she asked of Muffin.

"We met several times, often in this very room," he told her patiently, ignoring her pointed disapproval of the placement of his arms. "I am Sir Archibald Muffin, and I'm going to marry Phoebe."

"You are?" Phoebe asked softly, gazing up at him in adoration.

He nodded, then turned back to Lady Ffoulkes. "If Sir Giles is here, I will see him immediately."

Lady Ffoulkes was confused but not ready to lose control of the situation. "I think Cecil here was intending to speak to him, and he was here first."

"Oh, no," Cecil insisted, edging his way toward the door. "I was too late. Never even asked her. Sir Archibald was clearly ahead of me." He bowed to them all, and scurried out the door.

Lady Ffoulkes watched him go, then turned back to Muffin. "*Sir* Archibald Muffin, you say?" She looked pensive, as she tried to remember all she knew about his family and the size of his fortune. "As a matter of fact, Sir Giles is in the library right now, if you would like to speak to him."

She went to the door to lead him to Sir Giles, but Muffin wasn't ready to leave Phoebe.

"I'll be back to see you in a few minutes," he told her quietly. He looked down at Phoebe's red-rimmed eyes and hugged her closely. "Everything will be fine now," he assured her.

He bent down and kissed her gently on the lips, totally ignoring Lady Ffoulkes's impatient noises from the doorway. "You don't mind marrying me, do you?" he asked, a hint of his former uncertainty showing through.

"Oh, no," Phoebe sighed happily. "I would like to very much."

Muffin kissed her again, then sat her down on the sofa.

"Now, where is Sir Giles?" he asked Lady Ffoulkes impatiently, as if she had been keeping him waiting.

An hour later Phoebe burst into Julia's room. "Oh, Julia! I'm engaged!" she cried happily.

Julia had been expecting such an announcement, but had not thought it would be accompanied by such enthusiasm. She just stared at her sister.

Phoebe raced across the room and threw her arms around her sister, hugging her tightly. "Oh, it was so romantic! I think he would have challenged Cecil to a duel if I had asked him to!"

"What are you talking about?" Julia asked, thoroughly confused.

"Muffin!" Phoebe laughed, and letting go of Julia, bounced onto her bed. "He came back to see me. I had been so quiet when he left that he feared he had offended me in some way. He came back to beg my pardon for whatever it was he had done. Only he found me with Cecil," Phoebe covered her mouth and giggled. "I was crying."

"Why?"

"Because he was trying to propose. But Muffin thought he had done something evil. Oh, I never saw him so angry," she said, bouncing up and down. "I thought he was going to kill him."

Julia smiled even though she found it hard to

204

picture mild Muffin actually threatening anyone.

"Lady Ffoulkes came in," Phoebe continued. "And Muffin said he was going to marry me. Cecil was so relieved that he practically ran out the door. Muffin went to see Sir Giles, and it's all official." Phoebe hugged herself with joy. "I'm really going to marry him."

"I think it's wonderful," Julia said, sincerely glad that one of them would be happy.

"I can hardly believe it," Phoebe said, and promptly lost herself in her thoughts and wandered from the room.

After the door closed behind her, Julia was free to go back to what she had been doing. She looked down at the newspaper she held in her hand, and reread the advertisement that she had circled. It seemed to be an answer to all her troubles.

> Wanted, Companion: Must be young, healthy, willing to work hard. Needs to read well, and write a legible hand. Apply 5 Bedford Row.

It sounded like it might be just what Julia had been looking for. She didn't know where Bedford Row was, and knew it probably wasn't a fashionable neighborhood, but that hardly mattered. She pulled out a piece of writing paper and quickly wrote a letter of application.

After taking a few pence from her reticule,

Julia asked a footman to deliver it. He grinned conspiratorially as she gave him the coins and promised to deliver it safely. Julia suspected he thought he had been entrusted with a love letter.

CHAPTER TWELVE

The night had finally arrived for the grand party at Carlton House. It was to celebrate the Prince of Wales being made the regent, and more than two thousand people from the nobility and the gentry, along with the French royal family and foreign ambassadors, were invited.

For the past six weeks wherever the girls went they heard nothing but talk of this party. They felt very privileged to have been invited.

"It's really a shame that John cannot escort you," Phoebe said to Julia as Lady Ffoulkes's maid put the finishing touches on Julia's hairstyle. "I think he should have refused to go on duty tonight."

"A soldier can hardly refuse. It's his job," Julia pointed out. The maid finished arranging the small ringlets that fell softly down the side of her head, and placed two small, white satin flowers amid the curls. Once she stepped back, Julia went to her mirror. She could hardly believe that the girl she saw peering out at her was herself. Her white satin dress was cut simply, but had intricate embroidery in gold thread all along the bottom half of the skirt. On her ears flashed the small diamond earrings that matched her new necklace.

Lady Ffoulkes had given both her and Phoebe a set of diamond jewelry the night before. "There was money left from your clothing allowance," she shrugged when they tried to thank her. "Diamonds are a better investment than extra clothes."

Julia felt that the diamonds were just what was needed to complete her ensemble, and turned to Phoebe, quite satisfied with her appearance.

Phoebe's dress was very similar to her sister's, but was not such a simple style. She had embroidery, but not just along the bottom of the dress. It covered the neckline and the sleeves. She, too, had satin flowers in her hair. White ones, with streaks of gold thread running through them.

She wore her new diamond set, also, and had on her left hand an exquisite ruby and diamond engagement ring that Muffin had given her only that morning. He had ridden back to his estate to get his mother's ring. It had been in his family for years and he hoped that Phoebe would like it. He need not have worried. She loved it.

Julia was wearing no ring on her left hand. Apparently John had not thought to present her with a ring, but she was not upset by its absence. A ring would only make it all more real. She wasn't ever going to marry him, so there was no reason for him to waste his money on a ring that was supposed to stand for an emotion that wasn't present anyway.

"I don't really mind that John won't be there," Julia finally replied. "As long as you and Muffin don't mind if I tag along with you. John's been getting tiresome these last few days." Julia thought of how gloomy he had been and missed Phoebe's look of surprise. Phoebe seemed to think Julia had a strange attitude toward her fiancé.

"Oh, we won't mind at all," Phoebe hurried to assure her as she went to stand next to Julia at the mirror. They looked at their reflections together. "We both look beautiful," she laughed.

Julia nodded her head and laughed as she picked up her reticule. Phoebe began to chatter about the people she hoped to see that evening, but Julia was not listening to her. Her mind was on a letter she received from a Mrs. Hathaway. It was in reply to her letter of application for the job of companion. She wanted Julia to come for an interview the next morning, but Julia was suddenly filled with doubts. How could she slip out of the house unnoticed again? She had no idea where Mrs. Hathaway lived, for the street name was not familiar to her. How would she find her way?

Julia was terribly afraid that Mrs. Hathaway might not want to hire her, but equally apprehensive about what the future would hold if she did. She sighed as she and Phoebe walked down the stairs, wondering if she should just abandon her idea of a job and go ahead with the wedding. Perhaps if she hadn't been in love with someone else she could have married John, but being in love with Marc, she knew, in spite of all the misgivings about employment, that getting a job was the only thing for her to do.

Lady Ffoulkes and Sir Giles were waiting in the drawing room when the girls came down. With them was Muffin, and much to Julia's astonishment, Marc was also there. He looked terribly handsome in white satin knee breeches and a dark green velvet coat. Almost dangerously handsome, Julia thought, as he came forward to greet her.

"What are you doing here?" she asked. Her surprise at seeing him there made her forget her manners.

"John asked me to take his place and escort you tonight."

"That wasn't necessary," Julia panicked. She was quite embarrassed that John should do such a thing. And to have asked Marc, of all people! "I'm sure that you must have had other plans."

Marc looked at her in silence. No one else in the room seemed to be paying any attention to them. "I know that I'm the last one you would have chosen to take you to the party, but I could hardly refuse when Lyndon asked, so I suggest that we try to forget our differences and at least pretend to be enjoying each other's company."

Julia turned red at his slight reprimand and realized that her manners had been much at fault. "I didn't mean that I didn't want to go with you. I was just surprised, that's all," she tried to explain.

He nodded and squeezed her hand gently. "You don't have to make excuses to me. I know how you feel."

But you don't really, Julia thought as they left the house.

Carlton House was even more magnificent than Julia had imagined, and beside its splendor all her problems seemed insignificant. She was in awe of its richness and magnificence.

It was very crowded inside and Julia clung to Marc's arm. As he led her through the different rooms she asked him questions about everything. Marc looked down at her rather sadly. It was almost as it used to be before she had come to London, when he used to believe that one day she would be his. Now she was no longer the child he used to tease, but a beautiful woman who would belong to someone else in a short time. He sighed and squeezed her hand.

Julia looked up in surprise, but Marc was pointing out all the tables and chairs that had been set up in each room. "There are so many guests that they used almost every room, including the basements, to serve supper."

"Wouldn't it be funny to eat in the drawing room? Or the pantry? Or the wine cellar?" Julia laughed.

"We'll probably end up in the garden, since that's where most of the people will sit. There's only room for a few hundred inside."

He led Julia into the throne room whose walls were hung with deep red velvet on which were embroidered ornaments in gold thread. The canopy over the prince's throne was intricately carved out of wood and covered with gold. Four golden helmets were on the top with plumes of the finest ostrich feathers. On each side of the canopy magnificent draperies were hung that formed the background for several hung candelabra that lit the room. On the walls were large mirrors to reflect the light of the candles. They made the room seem full of light.

"It's beautiful," Julia sighed in awe. She had never seen anything like it.

"Ah, but there's more," Marc said, and led her through the door and across to the ballroom.

It was decorated with arabesque figures that had been painted on a gold background between the pilasters. The windows and recesses were decorated with rich blue velvet draperies with massive fringes, lace, tassels and ropes—all of gold. In the recesses were French plates of looking glass in gold frames, hung above sofas and chairs covered with blue velvet. In front of each pilaster had been placed a golden pedestal on which was a superb French girandole holding eight candles.

"This is even more beautiful," Julia said in wonderment.

"Do you think so? I prefer the throne room myself," Marc teased. "I was thinking of doing my sitting room at Worth Hall just like it."

Julia looked up at him in surprise, and he burst into laughter. "It may seem a bit pretentious to you," she pouted, "but I think it's magnificent."

"Magnificent, yes," he agreed with a smile. "But I'm not sure that I would want to live amid such elegance."

Julia shook her head slowly. "No, I guess I wouldn't either," she agreed.

"There's one room you must see," Marc said, and led Julia away once more. This time they went to the conservatory. "This is where the prince regent and his special guests will eat," he told her as they entered.

The conservatory was decorated in pink and silver, and was dominated by one long table that ran the entire length of the room. The upper end of the table was circular and had a splendid chair placed there for the prince. Behind it a huge medallion with the initials G.P.R. on it was hung on pink velvet drapes.

It was not all this splendor that caught Julia's eyes immediately, however. It was the circular basin of water that was set in the table at the prince regent's place with a small temple in the center of it. From this basin a meandering stream ran down to the end of the table. It was surrounded by green banks and spanned by three or four bridges, one of which had a small tower on it.

Julia looked at all this in silence, and Marc wondered what she thought of it all. Before he could ask, however, she slipped away from him and moved forward to get a better look.

As he came up next to her she pulled hurriedly at his sleeve. "Marc," she whispered, "there are fish in there."

Marc leaned closer and saw the small gold and silver fish swimming down the stream. He turned to see the laughter brimming in her eyes and hurried her out the door before she could actually laugh out loud.

"That's the prince's masterpiece," Marc cautioned her. "I think he'd be hurt if he knew you were laughing at it." He led her out into the garden and found a small alcove hidden by high bushes.

Julia looked up at him to see if he had meant what he said. She certainly did not want to insult anyone. Fortunately, Marc was laughing, too, by this time and found it impossible to sound stern.

"Why were there fish in the table?" she asked Marc.

"I think it was supposed to represent a garden."

"Then why doesn't he eat out here?" Julia asked, waving her hand at the rows of tables set up along the walks. She stopped suddenly. "Oh, but there may not be room for his temple."

"Or four bridges."

"Well, there surely are four bridges over the Thames, so why doesn't he just go out there," she laughed. "But I guess it just wouldn't be the same."

"No, I don't think it would be," Marc agreed. "It smells better in there, if nothing else."

Julia began to laugh again and failed to see a footman coming up behind her with a heavily laden tray. Marc pulled her to one side, but the sudden move surprised her and she almost lost her balance. Marc put out his other hand and steadied her quickly, but as he looked down into her eyes he forgot where they were and why he was with Julia.

The world all around them seemed to stop as they looked at each other. Julia was suddenly back at King's Rest, believing that Marc loved her. All of her own love for him shone in her eyes, and an unexpected desire to be in his arms brought a flush to her cheeks. She heard Marc inhale swiftly and felt his hold tighten as he pulled her closer to him. Her eyes closed as she waited for the touch of his lips on hers.

As she sensed him leaning down toward her

Julia suddenly felt Marc stiffen for the noises around them penetrated their isolation. Marc pulled away from her, letting his hands fall to his sides.

Julia turned away slightly as she opened her eyes, feeling curiously desolate and alone. She blinked rapidly, hoping to rid herself of the tears that were filling her eyes, and hoping that she had not given away her true feelings for Marc in those last few moments.

"I wonder what all the excitement is about," she said more calmly than she felt.

"I expect the prince has arrived." Marc strove for the same light conversational tone she had used. Damn! he said to himself. All she has to do is look at me and I forget everything. Including the fact that she's engaged to one of my good friends. I even imagine that I can see love in the way she looks at me. He shook his head disgusted with himself, and promised that he was not going to let his emotions betray Lyndon's trust in him again.

"We had better go in and meet the prince," he said, and solemnly led Julia back inside.

It seemed to take a considerable length of time before Julia was presented to the prince regent himself, and then she was rather disappointed, for he was not the magnificent figure she had imagined him to be. His scarlet coat, embellished with gold lace and set off by a brilliant star of the

Order of the Garter, only seemed to accentuate his portly figure and his red face. Julia tried to be impressed by him, but found that he looked like many other middle-aged men she had met in town.

After meeting the prince regent, she was introduced to the Comte de Provence and his family. She knew he was the dethroned Louis XVIII and was speechless in his presence, Luckily, he did not seem to expect conversation from her, and went on to someone else.

Dancing began about half past eleven, a fact for which Julia was particularly grateful. It meant that she would get some relief from Marc's company.

There was no actual complaint she could make about him. He was being attentive and courteous, but since the scene in the garden, Marc had been quite distant and cool toward her. Julia felt his change in attitude could be interpreted only one way: she had clearly revealed her feelings for him in the garden. He knew now that she loved him and was afraid that any slight lessening of the strict formal courtesy between them would be misunderstood by her.

Julia tried to look cheerful, but it was becoming harder and harder. Her only consolation was that this was the end of the season, and she would not have to put up this pretense any longer. With a little luck, in a few days she would begin her position as companion to the Mrs. Hathaway who had written her. She and Marc would go their separate ways, and it was quite likely that they would rarely, if ever, meet again. It was not the right thought to keep a smile on her face.

Marc danced with her once and woodenly performed all other duties required of him as her escort. He was trying to keep a tight rein on his emotions, but every time he saw Julia dancing with another man, he was burning with jealousy. He kept reminding himself of her engagement to Lyndon, but that did little to cool his raging anger.

Just who he was angry at, Marc didn't bother to ask himself, for it changed frequently. He was furious at any man who happened to dance with Julia, and equally angry with Julia if she happened to enjoy the dance. He was incensed with Lyndon for being engaged to Julia and infuriated with himself for ever allowing her to come to London before she was married to him.

Marc chanced to look across the floor at this point to see Julia laughing with the young man who was partnering her in a country dance. The thought of Julia enjoying herself with someone else so enraged him that he either wanted to thrash the fellow or throw about some of the damn statues the place was littered with. Instead, he turned on his heel and abruptly left, going out into the gardens even though the dance was coming to a close and he ought to be inside.

He quickly strode down a dimly lit path that took him away from Carlton House. He took deep breaths, telling himself all the while how foolish he was to get so overwrought. If he became so emotional when she merely danced with another, how was he going to get through her wedding? He shook his head, realizing it would have been better to stay away from her completely as he had tried to do once he had learned she was engaged.

Inside, Julia's young partner returned her to the settee where she and Marc had been sitting, but no one was there. She looked about in confusion, but the room was quite crowded and she saw no sign of him.

"Miss Henley," she heard a voice behind her say.

Julia turned around to see Sir Tristan waiting to speak to her. Her former partner looked at Julia questioningly, obviously anxious to find his next dance partner but unwilling to leave her unescorted.

"Hello, Sir Tristan," Julia said, and turned just in time to see the other man leaving. She turned back to Sir Tristan with a sigh. She did not really want to be alone with him, but she could hardly have demanded that the other man stay. She looked around for Marc again, but still saw no sign of him.

"You don't know how I've missed you," Sir Tristan was saying quietly, hoping to regain her wandering attention. "We must speak," he added urgently.

After her scene with Marc and her worries over her job interview, Julia was in no mood to play games with Sir Tristan. "I'm promised for the next dance," she told him politely, wondering which of the men wandering about the room was to be her partner.

"Then we must go someplace where we will not be disturbed." Before she could voice an objection, he took her arm and led her outside.

"Really, Sir Tristan, this is most improper," she protested. Where had Marc disappeared to? Wasn't he supposed to be nearby to prevent this very thing from happening?

"Oh, Miss Henley, you know I mean you no harm," he said smoothly. "I would do anything for you. Anything at all, for I just desire your happiness."

Julia was rather skeptical of his fancy phrases and wondered what promises he would make if he knew the true extent of her fortune. One phrase did stick in her mind, though. Anything at all? "There is just one little thing," she began.

"Just name it," he vowed dramatically. "Just give me any opportunity to prove my feelings for you."

"You see, I promised my old nurse that if I ever came to London, I would go to see her, and we've been here for more than a month and I just realized that I haven't made any attempt to see her."

Sir Tristan looked confused. "And just what would you like me to do?"

"I'm afraid I don't know how to find her street, and with all the rush of closing the house I hate to bother Lady Ffoulkes."

Sir Tristan's eyes narrowed. "You would like me to take you to see her?" he asked slowly.

"Oh, yes, if you could. Tomorrow morning if you're free."

"That would be fine," Sir Tristan murmured almost to himself. "Yes, it would be perfect." He turned to Julia. "I would be most happy to take you wherever you wish."

Julia smiled up at him. Now one worry was solved. She was sure that once she saw Mrs. Hathaway she would get the job. She'd beg, plead, agree to anything, so long as Mrs. Hathaway would hire her. She would slave away for a few pounds a year if it would save her from a loveless marriage.

Sir Tristan led her back to the doorway. He lifted her hand up to his lips. "Until tomorrow, my darling," he whispered much to Julia's surprise. "Then there will be no more good-byes." He kissed her hand lightly and disappeared into the house.

Good Lord, Julia thought as she stared after

him in astonishment. What idea had he gotten into his head now? All she had done was ask him to drive her some place. Did he see that as a sign of her undying love?

"So this is where you have gotten yourself off to!" Marc said as he suddenly loomed over Julia in a towering rage. "The minute you are out of my sight you sneak off with some man!"

Though she was startled by his sudden appearance, Julia could not help thinking he was being a bit unfair. She had been looking for him to help her escape from that very man. She had no chance to voice her protest, however, for Marc had her by the arm and was pulling her down the path he had just been walking on. Before they had gone very far, high boxwood hedges hid the canopied walkways and supper tables from their view. Marc turned around to face her.

"I'm expected to take Lyndon's place here tonight, but right in front of me you flirt with other men. You laugh with them and let them take you outside." Marc was so angry that the words seemed to spill out of him.

He reached out and grabbed hold of Julia's arms and shook her slightly. "What are you doing it for?" he asked.

Before she had a chance to answer, he pushed her away from him and strode a few feet along the path. He nervously ran his fingers through his hair and turned back to her. "Why did you agree to dance with them, anyway? You're engaged. I can remember that fact, even if you can't."

"What are you so angry about?" Julia finally had a chance to ask. "I haven't done anything wrong."

"What about being out here with Bentley? Don't you think that's going a bit beyond the bounds of propriety?"

"For your information, Marcus Cotsworthy," Julia said, advancing toward him, her hands on her hips and anger in her voice, "I did look for you when Sir Tristan approached me. I looked all over for you, but you were nowhere in sight."

Rather than appease Marc's anger, this only seemed to make it increase. "How disappointing for you that must have been," he said cynically. "I wasn't there to witness everyone paying court to the beautiful Miss Henley. What did you want to do? Gloat about how many men find you irresistible?"

Julia could not understand Marc's bitter anger. For some reason he seemed to feel that she was being unfaithful to John, at least that was what Julia assumed was causing the outburst. No matter how undeserving his criticism might be, just to have him angry at her hurt. "Please don't say those things, Marc," she pleaded as tears silently ran down her cheeks.

"Why not?" Marc continued. "I should think it would make you laugh to know that I'm still mad for you." He came closer, and in the dim light saw a silvery speck glide down her cheek. He reached out one finger and touched the tear. He stood silent and still, all of his anger fading as he looked down at her face.

"Oh, Julia," he whispered hoarsely, and gathered her in his arms. "I'm sorry, Julia," he murmured into her hair. "I didn't mean it."

His hand reached down gently and lifted her chin. He looked into her eyes for just a moment before his lips touched hers.

Julia had been kissed before, but never like this. His touch was gentle at first, but the passion that was so close to the surface broke through quickly. Her senses reeled and the world seemed to explode around them and then fade out of existence. She was clinging tightly to his coat, crushing the dark green velvet between her fingers. His hands caressed her back, pressing her ever closer to him, as if he wanted to feel the very beat of her heart next to his. Her lips parted at his insistence, and as his tongue began to explore her mouth, a shudder of pleasure went through her.

Suddenly, it was over. Marc was pushing her away from him. She realized to her shame that he was having difficulty doing it. Not because he was reluctant, but because she was clinging so tightly to him. With a start she pulled her hands away from the material as if it burned her. She was too embarrassed to even look at him.

"Julia," he said hoarsely. "I'm sorry."

She tried to shrug nonchalantly, pretending that the embrace had been pleasant but hardly earth shattering. "It's quite all right. It was partly my fault, anyway. I mean, I know you were angry because you thought I had forgotten about John." She realized that she was rambling and stopped abruptly.

"John," Marc moaned. "He trusted me, and look how I've repaid him. What can I ever tell him?"

"What do you need to tell him?" Julia asked, proud of her cool tone. "He doesn't really need to know about this any more than Claudia does. After all, it's not likely to happen again."

She felt Marc move closer to her, and she stiffened involuntarily, willing her treacherous senses not to betray her again.

"You know about Claudia?" he asked quietly.

"Oh, yes," Julia said brightly. "She told me herself."

"And you still . . . ?"

"Please, Marc. I don't want to talk about it," Julia interrupted. It would be far too humiliating to have to admit that she knew he was in love with someone else and yet had still let him kiss her like that. "Don't you think we ought to get back to the others?"

"Julia? Marc? Is that you?" Phoebe's voice called out from further down the path. In a moment she and Muffin had joined them. "It's time for supper," Phoebe said, totally unaware of the tension around her. "We were supposed to sit together. Did you forget?"

"No," Julia laughed, and went over to take her sister's arm. Together they started back down the path. "I'm just famished and was about to come and drag you two to the table whether you were ready to eat or not."

It was not difficult to stay out of Marc's way for the rest of the evening, for soon after supper was finished, Lady Ffoulkes and Sir Giles were ready to return home. Julia managed to chatter happily in the coach going home, safe in the knowledge that since they were not alone, no mention of the disastrous encounter would be made.

Once they were in the house, Julia said her good-byes quickly and raced up to her room. The darkness and the silence were what she needed. She slumped down on the floor next to her bed and cried. She cried until no more tears would come. Strangely enough, Julia felt a curious sense of peace as she pulled off her crumpled dress and climbed into bed. She only had one thought before she fell into an exhausted sleep. Would the pain of loving Marc ever disappear?

CHAPTER THIRTEEN

Phoebe opened the door to the sitting room and found Julia staring out the front window, obviously dressed to go out.

"Oh, Julia. You're dressed already." She frowned at the clock on the mantelpiece. "It's not time to leave for another hour."

Julia let the gold brocade drapery fall back in front of the window as she turned to face her sister. "It's not time to go where?" she asked. "I'm ready to go out driving with Sir Tristan."

Phoebe's eyebrows raised questioningly. "Out with Sir Tristan when you are engaged to John? Really, Julia," she teased. "Aren't you coming to the park with us, then?"

Julia remembered with a sigh that there had been talk of a trip to Hyde Park today. Since it was to be their last day in London, Phoebe had decided they should all meet for one last drive together. Marc had promised to relay the plan to John, while Julia had urged him to bring Claudia.

227

"Why would she want to come?" he had asked, perplexed.

"It'll be the last time we're together," Phoebe had said. "Of course she'll want to come."

But as Julia stood in the drawing room waiting for Sir Tristan, she wished the plans had never been made. She had had enough problems with her emotions last night and had no desire to be made to watch Marc and Claudia together. "I'll ask Sir Tristan to bring me to the park to meet all of you later," she agreed reluctantly.

"Good," Phoebe said. She looked at Julia's pale yellow muslin gown and the straw bonnet trimmed with white flowers and yellow ribbons. "Are you trying to make John jealous, or do you hope to captivate Sir Tristan?"

Julia looked down at her dress with a sigh. She had decided against her old black dress since Sir Tristan was driving her. She didn't think that going to see her old nurse would be a reason to dress like a drudge, so she chose what she thought to be her plainest dress. It was a simple style and a serviceable material. Unfortunately, it was also a flattering color and did much to emphasize her attractiveness. She hoped that Mrs. Hathaway would not view her as unsuitable because of it.

"I could hardly refuse to go driving with him when he asked me," Julia said as she turned back to the window. "He has been very nice to us while we've been here."

Phoebe nodded, but still cherished hopes of a romance between Julia and Sir Tristan. "He has been very attentive to you."

"Yes, because you led him to believe that I had a fortune," Julia said, glancing at the clock again. "I do wish he'd get here."

"What are you talking about? I never said you had a fortune. Why would that interest him, anyway?"

"You made several remarks when we first met him about the extent of grandfather's wealth. Then Lady Ffoulkes saw us together once and warned me that he's looking for money."

"How terrible!" Phoebe cried. "I don't believe it! He's far too gentlemanly and sincere."

Julia shook her head. "No, we're too trusting. But you needn't worry. I never had any hopes about him."

But Phoebe had, and she was not willing to abandon them so easily. "I don't think it's fair to listen to gossip. Everyone might be wrong about him, you know."

"Ah, here he is." Julia ignored Phoebe's comments and began to pull her gloves on. She thought again how fortunate she was that Sir Giles and Lady Ffoulkes were both out this morning, for she hadn't relished the thought of sneaking out of the house and trying to waylay Sir Tristan before he came to the door. She looked up as the butler showed him into the drawing room.

"You are looking beautiful today, as always," Sir Tristan said as he kissed Julia's hand. Julia looked pointedly at Phoebe, but her sister just smiled at them both, sure that Sir Tristan was too handsome to be devious.

"I was surprised that your sister wasn't coming also," Sir Tristan said as they pulled away from the house.

Julia remembered in time that she was supposed to be visiting her old nurse, who would have taken care of Phoebe also. "She had other plans for this morning," Julia said, and gave him the address. She hoped it wasn't too far because she didn't want to be late for the interview.

Julia was shown into Mrs. Hathaway's parlor five minutes late. She tried to make excuses, saying they had trouble finding the street, but Mrs. Hathaway did not seem to be listening. She was short and very fat, and looked like she was about fifty years old. She was wearing a severe black dress and a lace cap that covered most of her gray hair. Her face seemed to be molded into a perpetual frown.

"You don't look like my idea of a companion," she said sharply, glaring at Julia who was still standing since she hadn't been offered a chair.

"Well, I never was one before," Julia hesitated.

"Why do you want to be one now?" Mrs. Hathaway barked. "I'm not paying you to be a social butterfly."

"No, I wasn't expecting that," Julia said nervously. "I'm quite willing to work." Mrs. Hathaway was obviously looking at Julia's dress, as if it disproved her last statement. "I've just had a season, you see. I could only afford one and I didn't get any offers, so I have to find a job."

Julia's explanation seemed to delight Mrs. Hathaway. "So you were one of those snobs who goes to parties all the time, were you?" she asked rather insultingly. "Were you at Almacks?" she asked with relish.

"No, I didn't get to London until just a few weeks ago and my guardian didn't think it was worth the trouble to get me a voucher."

Mrs. Hathaway looked disappointed. "How about Carlton House? Ever see the prince?"

Julia nodded. "I was there last night."

Mrs. Hathaway grinned unpleasantly. The idea of a companion from the higher levels of society seemed to appeal to her. "I never was invited to any of those places," she told Julia. "I've got more than enough money, but some people don't think I'm good enough. Think my money's not as good as theirs. Ever hear of Edmund Hathaway?"

Julia shook her head.

"He was one of the biggest men in the slave business," she said proudly. "And was my husband. That's where all this came from." She waved her hand around the richly furnished room.

Julia felt her stomach turn. "I thought slavery was illegal," she said.

"It is here," she shrugged. "But not everywhere. Edmund was doing well in the West Indies until he died last year." She waited a moment, staring at Julia who shifted uncomfortably under her scrutiny. "Well?" she asked. "Aren't you going to tell me that you wouldn't work for such dirty money?"

Julia wanted to walk out. She would have liked nothing better than to turn her back on this awful woman and leave, but this was her only chance of a job. If she didn't take it, she would be married to John at the end of the week. Besides, she thought suddenly, she wouldn't have to stay here forever. She could stay as long as she could tolerate it, then she would find something else.

"No," Julia made up her mind. "I still want the job."

Mrs. Hathaway stood up. "You should know what your duties will be. I'm no invalid and can take care of myself, but you'll read to me when I want you to and run errands for me." Julia nodded. "And you'll be responsible for my collections," she pointed to the tables and cabinets that were filled with small statues and curios. There seemed to be thousands of them. "I don't trust their care to the maids. Clumsy things. You'll dust them and be responsible for them. There are more in the drawing room and my sitting room upstairs."

Julia nodded, fleetingly wondering if marriage to John would be better than this drudgery.

"The salary is ten pounds a year," Mrs. Hathaway concluded. "When can you start?"

Ten pounds a year was not very much, Julia realized, remembering times that she spent twice that much on shawls and hats without blinking an eye. Those days were certainly gone. "I can start tomorrow," she said.

Mrs. Hathaway nodded happily, and Julia let herself out the door. Sir Tristan was waiting outside, and she forced herself to look pleased with her visit.

"Have a nice chat?" he asked as he helped Julia up into his curricle. "Was she glad to see you?"

"Oh, yes. She was quite happy to see me," Julia said truthfully. "We had a very pleasant chat." She forced herself to smile but inwardly felt close to tears.

How long did she really think she would be able to stand being a companion to such a horrible person? What kind of life would she have once she left Sir Giles's house tomorrow?

Julia turned with a start as she realized that Sir Tristan had been speaking to her. "I'm sorry," she apologized prettily. "I didn't hear what you said."

Sir Tristan patted her hand. "Didn't I tell you not to worry? Didn't I promise that I would find a way?"

She just looked at him blankly, suddenly aware that they were pulling into an innyard. "What are we doing here?" she asked apprehensively.

A stableman ran up to the horses' heads. He held them while Sir Tristan jumped down, and then helped Julia do the same. "What are we doing here?" she asked again.

An older man came hurrying out of the stables. "What ken we do for ya, sir?"

"We're having a spot of trouble with the curricle," Sir Tristan said. "Do you have another carriage we might use?" Julia glanced at him quickly and could have sworn that he winked broadly at the man while he passed him a coin of some kind.

The man got a knowing look in his eye as he glanced at Julia. "Don't have much," he said to Sir Tristan, "but we ken find ya somethin'."

He and the stableman quickly unhitched Sir Tristan's horses and led them over to a closed carriage in the corner of the yard. Julia looked up at Sir Tristan who seemed strangely pleased with the whole affair.

In a matter of minutes he was helping Julia up into the other carriage, and after exchanging a few words with the stableman, climbed in after her.

"I don't really think this is proper," Julia protested.

"I was only thinking of your safety, my dear," he said mildly. "My curricle was clearly unsafe to drive in any further."

Julia had not noticed anything wrong with it, but she knew that she was far from an expert in such matters. She sighed and tried to relax. It couldn't be much further to Lady Ffoulkes's home.

Sir Tristan pulled back the shade slightly and glanced out as they moved along the streets. He said nothing for a while, and Julia became more and more uneasy.

"Aren't we almost there?" she finally asked.

Sir Tristan let the shade fall back into place, shutting off the small amount of light that it let in. The interior of the coach was surprisingly dim, which did nothing for Julia's nerves.

Suddenly she felt Sir Tristan beside her. He picked up her hand and clasped it tightly. "I promised you I'd find a way, and I have," he announced.

"A way for what?" Julia demanded, but her voice let her down and it came out as a whisper.

"For us to be married," he said, and took her into his arms. "My horses are fast and no one will be able to overtake us. In a few days we'll be in Gretna Green, and then we'll be together as we were meant to be." He paused to kiss her, but Julia moved just in time and his lips found only her cheek.

"Now, now, don't be shy," he laughed. "We have a long ride ahead of us. It'll give us plenty of time to get to know each other well."

Julia was quite terrified. Why hadn't she paid more attention to his vague promises instead of ignoring them? She should have made it quite clear that she had no fortune.

"But I don't want to elope with you," she cried, trying to be free of his hands.

"Then I shall just have to abduct you," he said calmly, reaching for her once again as the carriage jolted over the streets in its haste to leave the city.

CHAPTER FOURTEEN

"Just where can she be?" Marc asked them all for the twentieth time. He pulled his watch out of his pocket and looked at it again. "Why didn't she come with you?" he asked Phoebe.

Phoebe looked uncomfortable. After Julia left with Sir Tristan, she had begun to think about what Julia said, and feared there might be some truth in the matter. She did not want to upset John, though, by letting him find out that Julia was out riding with another man. She moved closer to Muffin and put her hand on his arm. "She had already left when Muffin came to get me," she admitted reluctantly.

"Where had she gone?" Marc asked impatiently.

Phoebe moved even closer to Muffin, glancing uneasily at John who didn't seem nearly as upset as Marc. "I don't really know what you're so upset about, you're not her fiancé."

Marc looked at her angrily, but could hardly dispute her words. John looked up suddenly. "I didn't know I was supposed to get her. I was calling on Claud—er, Miss Haywood this morning," he said.

Marc glanced at them both. "Well, she's not your responsibility. Julia is," he said tersely.

"Do you really think something's happened to her?" Phoebe asked Marc fearfully. She clung to Muffin's hand, as she noticed how worried Marc was. "I should never have let her go," she cried, becoming quite distraught.

Marc sighed with impatience, and Muffin took over. "Where did she go?" he asked Phoebe quietly. "If we knew, then we could make sure that nothing has happened to her."

"She just went for a drive with Sir Tristan," Phoebe said. "She said that he would bring her here to meet us."

"Bentley!" Marc spat out the name. "What the devil is she doing with him?"

Claudia gasped at Marc's language, and John took her arm protectively. "I think you ought to watch your language," John said. "There are ladies present."

"If you were less concerned with this lady and more concerned about your fiancée, maybe I wouldn't be speaking this way," Marc said.

Phoebe was really worried now. "Were all those things she said about him true?" she asked fearfully.

Marc turned back to her, thankful that Hyde

Park was so empty today. There were few people to witness their scene. "If it was something bad, then it probably was true," he said grimly. "How did she ever meet him?"

"We met him on our way to London," Phoebe admitted. "He seemed very nice, but Julia said he thought she had a lot of money."

"Why would he think that? Did she tell him that?" Marc asked.

"No," Phoebe hesitated. "She said that I gave him that impression," she said quietly. "So it's all my fault." She was obviously on the verge of tears, and Muffin put his arm around her shoulders.

"No, I'm sure it wasn't your fault," Marc softened, glancing briefly over at the lieutenant where he obviously thought some of the blame belonged. "Did she tell you where they were going to drive?"

Phoebe shook her head.

"I don't see what all the fuss is about," Claudia said suddenly. "It's not like he's going to abduct her in broad daylight."

Marc might have been sympathetic to Phoebe's distress, but he certainly did not share Claudia's opinion. "If you hadn't demanded Lyndon's company this morning, none of this would have happened," he told his cousin angrily.

Claudia's response was to burst into tears. John put his arm around her and tried to assure her that he placed no blame on her conduct, but she shrugged it off. "I don't see why you're all fussing over her," she sobbed. "Everyone's so concerned with precious little Julia, but no one cares about me." She turned and ran from the group, not caring where she went.

They all stood in shocked silence and watched as she ran across the lane that went through the park. It wasn't until a carriage was seen heading down the lane toward her that John suddenly came to his senses.

"Claudia!" he cried, and rushed after her.

Claudia stopped at the sound of his voice and saw the carriage rushing toward her. She watched as it came closer and closer, but fear had frozen her legs and she seemed unable to move. She was vaguely aware that the driver was trying to stop the horses, but her eyes were glued to their hooves as they pounded ever closer. Suddenly everything around her began to fade, and her last conscious thought was that perhaps now John would be sorry that he treated her so badly.

"You might have told me the truth," Sir Tristan pouted from across the carriage. The shades had been tied up and the carriage was filled with light. He looked so put out about the whole thing that Julia would have laughed had she not been so angry.

"I hardly make it a practice to announce the extent of my dowry to every man I meet," she pointed out. "Anyone who was truly interested could have approached Sir Giles."

Rather than comment on that, Sir Tristan looked out the window. "Can't that damn driver go any faster?" he muttered.

Julia smiled bitterly as she remembered Sir Tristan's reaction to the news that she had no fortune. He had been involved in what was supposed to be a passionate embrace when she managed to get the idea across to him. His passion died very quickly as he became the injured party. He accused her of trying to trick him, when he suddenly remembered that they were on their way out of London. He shouted for the driver to stop and turn around. Since then he had been sitting nervously, hoping they would avoid detection.

"We haven't been gone very long, have we?" he asked her again. "Your friends won't miss you yet, will they?" he said worriedly.

A small altercation with another carriage slowed them down, and he leaned out the window to shout curses at both his driver and the driver of the other viehicle.

Julia leaned back in her seat. It had been quite an eventful day. She suddenly became aware of a flower drooping in front of her face from her hat, and she took her bonnet off. It looked sadly crushed after Sir Tristan's last embrace.

"You've ruined my hat," she complained.

He looked uneasy. "Sorry," he muttered.

"I think you should buy me a new one," she said, thinking that her salary was not going to stretch to replacing hats. "You owe me that much, I think."

"I can't buy you a new hat," he snapped. "I don't have enough blunt to buy you a new handkerchief."

"No wonder you're in such a hurry to get me back before anyone notices my absence," Julia said. "Without a fortune, I'm a liability."

Sir Tristan glared at her. "You have a waspish tongue," he noted with distaste. "I never noticed that before."

"A lack of fortune makes all our faults more noticeable," she said uncharitably. She glanced outside. "Is this the park?"

Before Sir Tristan could answer, they heard a scream, and the coach was brought to an abrupt halt. Sir Tristan scrambled out, and Julia followed quickly.

In front of the horses stood John holding an unconscious Claudia in his arms. The driver slid down his seat.

"I dinn't hit 'er, sir. I swear. I dinn't hit 'er."

Marc saw Julia arrive and rushed to John's side. He should be with Julia, not Claudia. "For God's sake, man, give her to me," he hissed at John, while trying to remove Claudia from his arms.

"No," cried John. "You don't care what happens to her. All this is my fault. If she's dead, I'll never forgive myself." He carried her over to the grass and laid her gently on the lawn. "Claudia," he whispered gently.

Marc tried to push him away from her as John grabbed her hand and began to pat it, trying to revive her. "Would you go over and see if your fiancée is all right!" Marc shouted. "Claudia has only fainted." What was poor Julia thinking when the man she loved, the man she was engaged to marry, was totally unconcerned about her welfare?

John was totally oblivious to Julia and Marc. He kept whispering Claudia's name and trying to get some response from her.

Julia watched the scene in total disbelief. No one cared a jot about her! She was the one who had been abducted, and Marc and John were fighting over Claudia. Her interview and the prospect of working for Mrs. Hathaway, plus the abduction, were just too much for her, so she did what any normal girl would do in the circumstances. She clutched her tattered bonnet and burst into tears.

"Oh, Julia. Are you all right?" she heard Phoebe ask as she hurried over to her sister's side.

Julia nodded and fell into Phoebe's arms where she cried quite comfortably for a few minutes.

"Maybe we ought to take her home," Muffin suggested, afraid that they would draw a crowd.

He put a firm hand under her elbow and began to lead her away.

Julia had managed to stop her tears and was wiping her cheeks with her handkerchief when Marc came rushing over. She put her handkerchief down and tried to smile at him, but he rushed past her, seemingly taking no notice of her at all.

"What have you done to the woman I love?" he demanded of Sir Tristan, grabbing him by the cravat. Marc had had enough of John. If he wouldn't go to Julia's defense, then somebody who really cared about her, namely himself, would. Maybe then she would see who loved her and who didn't.

"It was just a misunderstanding," Sir Tristan hesitated, trying to pry Marc's hands loose.

"A misunderstanding!" Marc shouted. "She could have been hurt!"

Julia looked over to where Claudia was. Apparently she had regained consciousness and was sitting up with John's help. It must be nice, Julia thought, to have one man to sit with you and another to go to your defense. She burst into tears again. "Can we please go home?" she sobbed again.

Firm hands helped her up into a carriage. "You'll hear from me about this, Bentley," she heard Marc call from surprisingly close by. Was he passing by on his way back to Claudia? She began to cry even harder.

Julia felt the coach begin to move as someone's arms went around her, letting her cry against his chest. His? she thought with a start. She sat up suddenly to see Marc sitting quite close to her. He took a clean linen handkerchief from his pocket and began to wipe her eyes very gently.

"Marc!" she cried, quite surprised. She looked about her in confusion. She wasn't sure who she expected to be with her, but it certainly hadn't been Marc.

"I know you would rather it was John here," Marc apologized. "But I'm sure that he'll come to see you later today."

Julia waved aside his reference to John. "I thought you'd want to stay with Claudia."

"Claudia?" Marc was surprised at her suggestion. "I've had enough of Claudia in the last few weeks," he said in disgust.

Julia's eyes narrowed as she looked closely at him. "That's a very strange remark to make about the person you love."

"What are you talking about?"

"Well, you told me that you had fallen in love with someone else," Julia said a trifle impatiently. "Since Claudia was the only one you ever spoke to, I assumed it was her."

"Goodness, no," Marc laughed shortly. "I am

definitely not in love with Claudia. I only told you that to make you jealous," he confessed. "I thought if I was not so available you might begin to appreciate me more. But look how it backfired. While I was waiting for you to fall in love with me, you went and fell in love with John." He laughed bitterly.

Julia frowned. "You mean all this time you were really in love with me?" She found that hard to believe. But then she remembered with a smile the way he kissed her at Vauxhall and last night at Carlton House. Maybe it wasn't so hard to believe.

"Who's Claudia in love with, then?" she asked in confusion.

Marc hesitated a moment. "She's in love with John," he said quietly, afraid that he was going to hurt her.

"So that's who it was," Julia laughed. "I must say, I never guessed it was her."

"You don't seem very upset to learn that someone else is in love with your fiancé."

"Oh, she's quite welcome to him if she really wants him," Julia said generously. "I never really did, you know." Marc looked at her in astonishment. "You see, Lady Ffoulkes forced him into proposing to me because she found us together. It was all very innocent," she hastened to assure him. "But she was so anxious to marry us off to someone that she chose John because he was handy."

"Then you were lying when you said that you

were in love with someone?" Marc asked hopefully.

Julia looked at him a moment, remembering all the worries and fears she had had while he was trying to make her jealous. She was not quite ready to forgive him. "No," she said deliberately. "I have fallen in love."

Marc looked so crestfallen that she wanted to throw herself in his arms, but held back, with a secret smile.

"I assume you're going to break with John, then," Marc said quietly.

"Oh, yes," Julia said. "I think he should be able to be with Claudia. I think anyone who really loves someone ought to have the chance to be with that person," she added cryptically.

Marc nodded sadly, and turned to look out the window. "I suppose the man you love will be quite happy to hear that you're free now."

"I hope so," she said, smiling at him from the corner where she sat. But he didn't see, for he was still staring out the window.

"I wasn't sure that he cared for me until just recently," she said casually, but Marc still made no response. "I may have to push him a bit to get him to marry me, though."

Marc still gazed out the window, while Julia fidgeted impatiently. She was reluctant to come right out and tell him that he was the one she loved, and had hoped that he would take some of her hints. She nervously tapped her foot against the seat, realizing that every second was bringing them closer and closer to Sir Giles's house.

"Do you realize that it's most improper for us to be in this closed carriage together?" she asked conversationally.

Marc looked over at her. "You know that I'm not going to hurt you," he said, and turned back to the window.

I can see that, Julia thought in disgust. She sighed loudly, but that got no response, either. "If Lady Ffoulkes sees us, she'll put the wrong interpretation on things," Julia told him. "My reputation will be gone." Was she going to have to come right out and tell him that she loved him after all?

"Oh, Julia," Marc said in exasperation. "You are getting out of one engagement you were forced into. You certainly don't want to get into another because of compromising circumstances. Why look for trouble? Give this man of yours a chance to propose."

"I've been trying to, but he's remarkably dense," Julia said. She crossed her arms and leaned back, glaring at him.

Marc looked at her for a moment in silence. A smile suddenly spread over his face, as she began to smile in return. "You little minx," he whispered as he reached over for her.

No longer able to restrain herself, she threw

herself into his arms. "Oh, Marc, I do love you so," she said shyly.

He leaned down and kissed her quite thoroughly. Her arms somehow found their way around his neck, and she clung quite shamelessly to him.

After a few minutes the stillness of the carriage penetrated Marc's consciousness. "I think we're at your house," he said, and pulled slightly away from her.

Julia stared at him a moment before his words made any sense to her. "Oh," she said, and turning a bright red, took her arms away.

Marc leaned over and kissed her quickly on the forehead, then opened the carriage door. "You've led me quite a dance, you know," he teased her as he helped her down. "It would have served you right if you had ended up married to John."

"I wouldn't have," Julia assured him. "Oh, dear," she said, putting her hand over her mouth. "I forgot all about Mrs. Hathaway."

"Who's Mrs. Hathaway?" Marc asked.

"I'm supposed to be her companion starting tomorrow," Julia said quietly. Marc was frowning at her, so she went on rather quickly. "I didn't want to marry John, or anyone else, since I was in love with you, so I got myself a job. As a companion." His expression was quite forbidding, so she looked down at her shoes. "She wasn't very nice, but I accepted the job because I didn't know what else I could do. She can't make me work for her now, can she?" she asked fearfully.

When Marc didn't answer, she looked timidly up at him. His expression was stern but not exactly angry. "So that's another sin to be laid at my door because of my stupid ideas," he said, not upset with Julia but quite angry at himself for causing her more worries.

Julia was just staring at him blankly, not understanding what he was talking about, so he hugged her quickly. "Never mind all that," he said. "Just give me her address and I'll take care of her."

He took her arm and led her up the steps to the house. Before they had a chance to knock, Lady Ffoulkes pulled the door open and was glaring down at them. "Julia! What do you think you are doing riding in a closed carriage like that? What will Lieutenant Lyndon think?"

"Since I've decided not to marry him, I don't really care what he thinks," Julia shrugged as she went past her into the house.

"But, Julia, your reputation," she wailed. Turning suddenly to Marc, she said seriously, "I suppose you realize how you have compromised Julia by bringing her home in that carriage. Why all the neighbors must have seen it," she added, conveniently forgetting the fact that most of the neighbors had left town already.

"It's all right," Marc said. "I'm quite prepared

to sacrifice myself and make an honest woman of her."

Lady Ffoulkes was not sure how to take his remark, but since he was agreeing to marry Julia, she overlooked the hint of levity that had no place in their conversation. Julia, however, was not so agreeable and looked daggers at him.

Marc only laughed and swooped her up into his arms. "Didn't I always say you'd be mine one day?" he laughed.

Dell Bestsellers

- [ ] TO LOVE AGAIN by Danielle Steel $2.50 (18631-5)
- [ ] SECOND GENERATION by Howard Fast $2.75 (17892-4)
- [ ] EVERGREEN by Belva Plain $2.75 (13294-0)
- [ ] AMERICAN CAESAR by William Manchester ... $3.50 (10413-0)
- [ ] THERE SHOULD HAVE BEEN CASTLES
  by Herman Raucher $2.75 (18500-9)
- [ ] THE FAR ARENA by Richard Ben Sapir $2.75 (12671-1)
- [ ] THE SAVIOR by Marvin Werlin and Mark Werlin . $2.75 (17748-0)
- [ ] SUMMER'S END by Danielle Steel $2.50 (18418-5)
- [ ] SHARKY'S MACHINE by William Diehl $2.50 (18292-1)
- [ ] DOWNRIVER by Peter Collier $2.75 (11830-1)
- [ ] CRY FOR THE STRANGERS by John Saul $2.50 (11869-7)
- [ ] BITTER EDEN by Sharon Salvato $2.75 (10771-7)
- [ ] WILD TIMES by Brian Garfield $2.50 (19457-1)
- [ ] 1407 BROADWAY by Joel Gross $2.50 (12819-6)
- [ ] A SPARROW FALLS by Wilbur Smith $2.75 (17707-3)
- [ ] FOR LOVE AND HONOR by Antonia Van-Loon .. $2.50 (12574-X)
- [ ] COLD IS THE SEA by Edward L. Beach $2.50 (11045-9)
- [ ] TROCADERO by Leslie Waller $2.50 (18613-7)
- [ ] THE BURNING LAND by Emma Drummond $2.50 (10274-X)
- [ ] HOUSE OF GOD by Samuel Shem, M.D. $2.50 (13371-8)
- [ ] SMALL TOWN by Sloan Wilson $2.50 (17474-0)

At your local bookstore or use this handy coupon for ordering:

Dell DELL BOOKS
P.O. BOX 1000, PINEBROOK, N.J. 07058

Please send me the books I have checked above. I am enclosing $_____
(please add 75¢ per copy to cover postage and handling). Send check or money order—no cash or C.O.D.'s. Please allow up to 8 weeks for shipment.

Mr/Mrs/Miss _____

Address _____

City _____ State/Zip _____

INTRODUCING...

Romantique

The Romance Magazine For The 1980's

Each exciting issue contains a full-length romance novel — the kind of first-love story we all dream about...

PLUS

other wonderful features such as a travelogue to the world's most romantic spots, advice about your romantic problems, a quiz to find the ideal mate for you and much, much more.

ROMANTIQUE: A complete novel of romance, plus a whole world of romantic features.

ROMANTIQUE: Wherever magazines are sold. Or write Romantique Magazine, Dept. C-1, 41 East 42nd Street, New York, N.Y. 10017

Romantique

INTERNATIONALLY DISTRIBUTED BY DELL DISTRIBUTING, INC.

Love—the way you want it!

Candlelight Romances

		TITLE NO.	
☐ THE CAPTIVE BRIDE by Lucy Phillips Stewart	$1.50	#232	(17768-5)
☐ FORBIDDEN YEARNINGS by Candice Arkham	$1.25	#235	(12736-X)
☐ HOLD ME FOREVER by Melissa Blakeley	$1.25	#231	(13488-9)
☐ THE HUNGRY HEART by Arlene Hale	$1.25	#226	(13798-5)
☐ LOVE'S UNTOLD SECRET by Betty Hale Hyatt	$1.25	#229	(14986-X)
☐ ONE LOVE FOREVER by Meredith Babeaux Brucker	$1.25	#234	(19302-8)
☐ PRECIOUS MOMENTS by Suzanne Roberts	$1.25	#236	(19621-3)
☐ THE RAVEN SISTERS by Dorothy Mack	$1.25	#221	(17255-1)
☐ THE SUBSTITUTE BRIDE by Dorothy Mack	$1.25	#225	(18375-8)
☐ TENDER LONGINGS by Barbara Lynn	$1.25	#230	(14001-3)
☐ UNEXPECTED HOLIDAY by Libby Mansfield	$1.50	#233	(19208-0)
☐ CAMERON'S LANDING by Anne Stuart	$1.25	#504	(10995-7)
☐ SUMMER MAGIC by F.C. Matranga	$1.25	#503	(17962-9)
☐ LEGEND OF LOVE by Louis Bergstrom	$1.25	#502	(15321-2)
☐ THE GOLDEN LURE by Jean Davidson	$1.25	#500	(12965-6)
☐ MOONLIGHT MIST by Laura London	$1.50	#263	(15464-4)
☐ THE SCANDALOUS SEASON by Nina Pykare	$1.50	#501	(18234-4)

At your local bookstore or use this handy coupon for ordering:

Dell | **DELL BOOKS**
P.O. BOX 1000, PINEBROOK, N.J. 07058

Please send me the books I have checked above. I am enclosing $ _____
(please add 75¢ per copy to cover postage and handling). Send check or money order—no cash or C.O.D.'s. Please allow up to 8 weeks for shipment.

Mr/Mrs/Miss _____

Address _____

City _____ State/Zip _____

**Sometimes you have to lose
everything before you can begin**

To Love Again
Danielle Steel

Author of *The Promise* and
Summer's End

Isabella and Amadeo lived in an elegant and beautiful world where they shared their brightest treasure—their boundless, enduring love. Suddenly, their enchantment ended and Amadeo vanished forever. With all her proud courage could she release the past to embrace her future? Would she ever dare TO LOVE AGAIN?

A Dell Book $2.50 (18631-5)

At your local bookstore or use this handy coupon for ordering:

Dell **DELL BOOKS** To Love Again $2.50 (18631-5)
P.O. BOX 1000, PINEBROOK, N.J. 07058

Please send me the above title. I am enclosing $ _____
(please add 75¢ per copy to cover postage and handling). Send check or money order—no cash or C.O.D.'s. Please allow up to 8 weeks for shipment.

Mr/Mrs/Miss _____

Address _____

City _____ State/Zip _____

THE PASSING BELLS

by

PHILLIP ROCK

A story you'll wish would go on forever.

Here is the vivid story of the Grevilles, a titled British family, and their servants—men and women who knew their place, upstairs and down, until England went to war and the whole fabric of British society began to unravel and change.

"Well-written, exciting. Echoes of Hemingway, Graves and *Upstairs, Downstairs*."—*Library Journal*

"Every twenty-five years or so, we are blessed with a war novel, outstanding in that it depicts not only the history of a time but also its soul."—*West Coast Review of Books*

"Vivid and enthralling."—*The Philadelphia Inquirer*

A Dell Book $2.75   (16837-6)

At your local bookstore or use this handy coupon for ordering:

| Dell | **DELL BOOKS**   THE PASSING BELLS $2.75   (16837-6)
 P.O. BOX 1000, PINEBROOK, N.J. 07058 |

Please send me the above title. I am enclosing $ _____
(please add 75¢ per copy to cover postage and handling). Send check or money order—no cash or C.O.D.'s. Please allow up to 8 weeks for shipment.

Mr/Mrs/Miss _____

Address _____

City _____ State/Zip _____